MEGGIE & MAX

NOVELLA TWO

BARRINGTON SERIES

SUSAN MACKIE

*small town
publishing*

FOREWORD

While the town of Barrington does exist, it is just a small village with a general store.

I've imagined elements of nearby larger towns, such as Gloucester, to create the township of Barrington for this story.

Any similarities to people, living or deceased, are purely co-incidental and a product of my imagination.

The Barrington Tops, Bucketts Mountain, Barrington and Gloucester rivers do exist and it is a stunning region to visit.

MEGGIE & MAX

He's the new Vet with something to hide. She's got a wedding to organise.

Meggie's in Barrington for her brother's wedding, local Vet Angus Hamilton. After working overseas for years, she hasn't told her family she's not going back. And she hasn't told them why.

Max is the Locum Vet hired to help out in the lead up to the wedding and during the honeymoon. But he doesn't arrive alone.

They each need to move on from their past. When their secrets are revealed, will it empower them, or tear them apart?

MEGGIE & MAX

SUSAN MACKIE

For Marion (Mum)

*and all the wonderful folk who keep
small town communities
alive and thriving.*

Susan Mackie

1

'We're here Sis. Barrington Homestead.'

Meggie opened her eyes, stretched, then grinned at her brother before turning to look through the windscreen. The car was still, although she could hear the engine running. Angus had stopped at the start of a long driveway, lined with poplar trees. The setting sun created a golden glow through the tall trees, and with a glimpse of the homestead in the distance she subconsciously ran her fingers through her thick, dark hair.

'Are you ready for this?' Angus winked before putting the car in gear. 'You'll love Rose, don't worry. It's wee Charlie that might test you.' His eyes crinkled at the corners. Meggie hadn't seen Angus for four years, but she loved how happy and settled he was, with his fiancée, Rose and their small son.

The paddocks on either side of the driveway were green and lush. They'd had good rain over the summer. The homestead was now fully in view. She'd seen pictures of course, but the dignified lines of the old home took her breath away. She saw Rose run lightly down the steps, waving as they pulled in. They'd spoken many times in the last few years and Meggie hoped the easy warmth they'd shared on the phone and in video catch-ups translated into real life. She could use a friend. A sister.

Rose was at the car door before they'd fully stopped, yanking it open as Meggie unfastened her seatbelt. Stepping out, Meggie was eye to eye with Rose for the briefest moment, before she was pulled into a tight embrace, Rose's cheek against her own. Meggie drew her breath in, then hugged her soon-to-be-sister-in-law back with the same degree of fierce, generous warmth. They took half a step back, still holding each other, then Rose pulled her in for another quick, tight, squeeze saying quietly, 'Oh Meggie, we're so happy you've come home. Welcome to Barrington.'

Meggie laughed, as Angus stepped between them, an arm around each of their shoulders. 'Now don't think for a moment that you girls can gang up on me. I've got little Charlie and Woof on my team, so that's three against two.'

Cattle dog Woof, hearing his name, promptly joined them, sitting at Rose's feet, his tail wagging madly against their legs. Meggie knelt down, patting the dog while she composed herself. They'd said she was welcome. Had been telling her so for months. And to stay as long as she liked. But she hadn't been sure if she'd *feel* welcome, she'd been overseas for years. But this was a good start. It was as if Rose knew exactly what she needed, in that moment. And Angus. Well Angus had always looked out for her. They'd been close growing up and she knew he'd welcome her. But he was getting married, and she wouldn't blame him if having her here would be complicated.

'Take Meggie in, show her the house. I'll bring the bags.' Angus opened the back of the red Jeep, hauling out two large suitcases. Meggie hadn't told them she wasn't returning to California. She was keeping that to herself a bit longer.

'Let me help you Gus. They're heavy. I almost exceeded the weight limit with those. But I do have some wine for you from the Napa Valley, so be gentle.' Meggie stepped toward him, but paused as Rose snorted, then laughed loudly.

'Gus? Really? Gus? Is that your nickname? Why do I not know this?' Still laughing, Rose was now bent over, holding her stomach. 'Wait until I tell the local lads this one. Oh, that's priceless.'

Meggie giggled too. It was her private name for Angus. Only their grandfather and Meggie had ever used it. One or two had tried at High School and been sorry afterwards, Angus hadn't taken their teasing lightly.

'Rose, where's Charlie? It's too late for nap time.' Angus changed the subject, then chuckled as Rose paled before racing up the stairs into the homestead without a word. Turning to Meggie, he said, 'Honestly, we can't leave him unsupervised for a moment. And well, if he's quiet, that's all the more worrying.' Meggie chuckled inwardly at the delight and pride on her big brother's face. Whatever little Charlie was up to would probably be fine by him. Meggie followed him up the stairs to the veranda, as Rose returned, flushed, holding two and a half-year-old Charlie on her hip. He had crumbs around his mouth, and something firmly gripped in his pudgy right hand.

'He was in the laundry.' Rose shook her head at Charlie who leaned back in her arms, his eyes focussed on the dog. 'Woof. Good Woof.'

'And is that dry dog food in his little hand there?' Angus shook his head in mock disgust, turning to Meggie. 'He likes sharing his food with Woof ....'

'Is that okay?' Meggie hesitated for a moment. 'That he's eating dog food?' She looked from Rose to Angus.

'Um. He's eaten worse. We have stories.' Rose shook her head, then beckoned Meggie. 'Come in, we'll show you the house. And you have the whole bed and breakfast section to yourself.' Rose lowered her voice. 'Charlie hasn't worked out how to get that door open yet, so you'll be safe.'

Meggie grinned, following them into the house. She stopped for a moment in the grand hallway. It's polished floors gleamed, a lovely warm contrast to the cream timber walls and white pressed metal ceiling. 'Welcome to Barrington Homestead.' Angus and Rose spoke together, little Charlie was now wriggling to get down. Meggie turned around, taking it all in. Yes, she did feel welcome.

Meggie looked at her brother and Rose. 'Thank you.' She said it quietly, but hoped it conveyed how grateful she was to be here, to be welcomed without question.

2

Max glanced at his watch. Almost an hour early. Good, he can stretch his legs and have a look at the town before his interview. Not an interview exactly, a meeting. He'd already committed to the Locum position at Barrington Vet Clinic for the full three months.

He'd been here before. Two winters ago a late cold snap had dropped several inches of snow in the Barrington Tops overnight. They'd followed a steady stream of vehicles from Newcastle to Barrington. So many happy families. They'd built a snowman, had a snowball fight and roasted marshmallows over a fire in a large drum while the children ran around, jumping in snowdrifts and making friends with strangers. It had been a really happy day.

Turning, he looked at Tommy, who was gazing around with interest at the locals coming and going.

'Ready mate?' Max pointed to a café on the other side of the road. 'We've got time for a milkshake if you're thirsty.'

Tommy didn't hesitate, undoing his seatbelt as he spoke. 'Okay. And maybe some cake?'

Max laughed, reached over and ruffled his son's hair. 'Is there ever a moment when you're not hungry?'

Pausing, Tommy seemed to consider his words. He grinned at his father. 'Nup. Always hungry. Unless its green stuff. Not so hungry for green stuff. Ever.'

Max laughed out loud, and Tommy joined in. It felt good. Natural. They couldn't grieve forever. Laughing was therapeutic. He'd read that somewhere. Noting the way Tommy's face lit up, Max knew they needed to laugh more. And to let Tommy know it's okay to be happy.

They walked across the road, busy for a small town on Friday afternoon. Max resisted the urge to hold Tommy's hand. His son had mentioned recently that eight-year-olds don't need their hands held.

Tommy bounced straight up to the counter, peering at the arrangement of cakes and slices. Standing behind him, Max smiled at the woman cleaning the coffee machine.

'Afternoon. Is it too late to get a milkshake and a coffee? We can choose something from the drinks cabinet if you're already cleaning up for the day.' He wanted to start off on the right note in this town. Although he'd almost kill for a coffee right now.

'No problem at all. What would you like?'

Her smile was warm, and he nodded, pleased. Something loosened a little in his chest. He turned to Tommy. 'Come and order son. Tell the lady what you'd like.'

Tommy grinned at his father before turning to the woman. 'A chocolate milkshake. And a piece of apple pie please.' Max was about to speak when Tommy continued. 'And Dad will have a large double shot Americano. With a lid please.'

'I like a customer who knows what he wants. I'll get that started straight away. Why don't you take a seat and I'll bring it out in a moment. Would you like cream or ice cream with your apple pie?' The woman was warm and friendly. And obviously used to children.

'Both please. And two spoons.' Tommy looked earnestly at the lady. 'I'm trying to fatten Dad up a bit.'

Max snort-laughed and nudged Tommy with his elbow. Seeing Tommy relaxed and making jokes almost choked him up.

'Two spoons it is then.' She was chuckling too and somehow it felt like this little town had just made them welcome.

They sat at a table on the pavement. Max could see the sign for the Vet clinic further down the street. So the café would be his local for the next three months. Good. Tommy was reading shop signs, asking questions and generally being more communicative than he had in months. Max relaxed.

'Well I see you've picked out the best table for people watching. Here's your milkshake.' She leaned toward Tommy as she placed it on the table. 'There's an extra shot of chocolate in it, you let me know if it's okay, won't you.' Tommy said yes quickly, half-standing to reach the straw with his mouth, taking such a big sip his cheeks were sucked in.

Smiling broadly, she placed the coffee in front of Max, and set the large slice of pie between them, with two spoons and forks. 'I'm Debbie by the way.'

Tommy swallowed. 'I'm Tommy. Best. Milkshake. Ever.'

He picked up a spoon, then remembered his manners. 'Thank you Debbie. This is my dad, Max.'

Max held out his hand, taking Debbie's slender one in his. 'Nice to meet you Debbie. It seems your milkshake has the Tommy Masters tick of approval.' He watched as Tommy nodded his head enthusiastically, a bite of apple pie already in his mouth.

'Well that's good news. Let me know if the pie gets the Tommy Masters tick too. Our baker, Cathy, will want to know.'

Tommy was nodding and chewing but pushed the plate closer to Max. Picking up a spoon, Max took a large bite, closing his eyes for a moment as the pastry melted in his mouth and the fresh apple and cinnamon taste hit the back of his tongue. His eyes widened. He realised, as he did, that he hadn't been tasting food for months. Oh, he'd been eating. But not enjoying. Not tasting. The pie was good, really good. He looked up at Debbie. 'Best. Pie. Ever.' She laughed and returned to the kitchen. Max watched her. She thought he was being polite but damn it, he meant it.

3

Meggie stretched and rolled onto her back. She'd slept well. Angus had insisted she have dinner with them and stay up, only letting her go to bed when they did, to overcome jetlag. He was right, she'd slept right through the night and felt rested. She picked up her phone. Almost seven, she was sure Angus would be up. He'd said last night he'd feed the horses and check the cattle before he went to the clinic.

Dressed in shorts and a tank top with her long dark hair in a high ponytail, already feeling the warmth of the Australian summer, Meggie walked from her quarters to the door of the main house. She didn't want to wake Rose and Charlie, so she opened the door softly. Stepping into the hallway she could smell something cooking. Toast? Walking quietly along to the kitchen she paused. Rose was speaking to someone.

'And you're going to eat your eggs with the spoon. Not

your fingers. The spoon. See, like this.' Meggie stepped into the room. Rose had a tea towel over her shoulder and a splatter of something, vegemite perhaps, on her tee shirt. Her face was flushed and ponytail lop-sided. Charlie was perched in his high-chair, a Sippy cup in front of him and what looked like scrambled eggs and pieces of sausage. He had vegemite all over his cheek and the child-size fork firmly clutched in his chubby hand.

'Morning Rose, Charlie.' Meggie kissed her nephew on the top of his head, then patted his ginger hair, before walking across to Rose.

'Morning Meggie. Did you sleep okay?' Rose picked up the electric jug. 'Tea? I usually get a coffee from Deb's when I go into town.'

'Best sleep I've had in ages. I'll pour myself a glass of water, thanks Rose. Coffee in town sounds perfect.' Meggie glanced out the window. 'It's going to be warm, I've got to get used to the heat again.' She watched as Rose wiped Charlie's hands and face with a damp cloth, then lifted him out of the high-chair. He ran to a large mat in the living area covered with wooden blocks and farm animals and promptly sat down, absorbed in a game of his own making.

Rose pulled up a stool to the kitchen bench, patting the one next to her for Meggie. 'We are so pleased to have you home. Thank you for making the trip.' Rose took a sip of her tea. 'Your Mum will be here in a few weeks for the wedding, I'm sure she can't wait to see you.'

'I'm happy to be home Rose. I think I've been away long enough.' Meggie glanced outside, she could see Angus striding toward the house, Woof trotting beside him. Looking back at Rose she added softly, 'I'm not sure I want to go back, Rose. I think my time there is over.'

If Rose was surprised, she didn't show it. 'Help me get this wedding organised and done, and then think about what you want to do next.' She stood as Angus walked in. He kissed Rose full on the mouth, then grinned at his sister, giving her a wink.

'Megs. Sleep okay?' He picked Charlie up, settling him on his hip. 'What have you been up to Charlie?'

'Great sleep, thanks Gus.' She sat back as Angus bustled around the kitchen, his son still in his arms while he fixed himself a bowl of cereal. Setting Charlie back on the floor, Angus leant over his bowl, spoon in hand. Charlie wandered back to his blocks.

Loving the way Rose and Angus responded to each other, chatting about their horses and cattle, their plans for the day, was relaxing for Meggie. Her tourism job had been hyper busy, dealing with events, demanding clients, temperamental chefs, overwrought brides and more recently a disintegrating relationship with her boss. Whatever she did next, she knew it would never be as stressful as her work in Napa Valley.

Meggie and Rose cleaned up the breakfast dishes while Angus went to shower before going into town to open the Vet Clinic.

'He's got a meeting this afternoon with a Locum Vet. If all goes well he'll start next week, staying for three months while we prepare for the wedding and have a brief honeymoon after.' Rose paused, glancing at Charlie, still playing on the floor. 'Angus works such long hours and does a lot of travelling around the district. I've asked him to consider an employee, maybe a future partner in the practice, so he can be home a bit more.'

'So this Locum will stay longer if it works out?' Meggie was curious.

'I don't think Angus has discussed the possibility of ongoing work. He wants to see how the fellow, Max, is with the locals. He's had considerably more small animal experience than large, coming from Newcastle, but has indicated a keen interest in equine health.' Rose let the water out of the sink, leaned her back against it, her expression unsure.

'There's more. Angus wants another baby. Before Charlie gets too much older.' She frowned slightly as she looked at Charlie, now stacking wooden blocks up into a tall, wobbly tower.

'And you don't?' Meggie wasn't sure if she should ask, but Rose had started the conversation.

'I do. Really I do. But Charlie is a handful and I've asked Angus to consider changing the way he works, to be home more.' A flush had crept up Rose's neck and Meggie reached out, touching her shoulder for a moment.

'What is it Rose? What's holding you back?'

Rose sighed. 'I've always been a strong, independent woman. Thought I could do anything I set my mind to. But having Charlie. Well. He's flipped some sort of a switch in me. I'm softer somehow.' She grinned sheepishly at Meggie. 'That's not a bad thing. But it's also made me a bit, I don't know, clingy. It's not the right word, but when Angus works long hours I resent it. I feel like I'm raising Charlie on my own at times. I'd like him home more. Running the farm together. Taking Charlie outside to do farmer-stuff when he can.' Rose took a deep breath. 'If we can get someone to handle the Vet Clinic in town most days, Angus could almost run the large animal work from here. He'd still have to go out to farms…' She trailed off, looking up.

Meggie turned to see Angus striding towards them in a clean shirt and jeans, his hair damp from the shower.

'What are your plans today Megs? Want to come into town and have a look around?' Angus wrapped his arm around her shoulders, giving her a brotherly squeeze. 'It'll be a bit slower than you're used to, but it's a great little town. What do you say? Want to ride in with me?'

Meggie nudged him with her elbow, dislodging his arm. 'I've already got a check-out-Barrington date, Gus. I'm riding in with Rose and Charlie.'

'Oh, I see how it is. The girls *are* ganging up on me.' Angus grinned at both women.

'There's coffee involved. Rose promised coffee.' Meggie laughed at his expression. 'Go Angus. I'll drop into the Clinic later, I'd love to see it.'

Angus kissed Rose and turned toward the door. Suddenly Charlie let out a wail, getting to his feet he ran toward Angus, arms in the air, knocking his tower of blocks flying as he went.

'Daddeeee, daddeee!' Rose scooped him up into her arms, but he wriggled, arms still out, trying to get to his father. Angus tousled Charlie's hair. 'Gotta go buddy, be good for Mummy and Meggie.'

Mouthing 'sorry' to Rose, Angus shot out the door. Rose patted Charlie's small back, now sobbing against her shoulder as if his heart would break. 'Daddeee! Want Daddee!'

Rose rocked back and forth, making soothing noises. Meggie picked up Charlie's Sippy cup, holding it out to him. He looked at her suspiciously before taking the cup in his hands, sipping in between sobs. It was a full five minutes before his tears subsided and Rose could set him back down with his toys.

Meggie raised her eyebrows at Rose. 'And this happens, how often?'

'Every day. Every bloody day.' Rose looked fondly at Charlie. 'He's often in bed when Angus gets home. Especially if he's been in the clinic most of the day, then gets a call out to a property. Sometimes he's gone in the morning before Charlie wakes up. This is what I mean. He needs Angus to be here a bit more. We both do.' She sighed.

'Oh Rose, I totally see what you mean. Let's hope this guy, Max, works out. Maybe he's the answer.' Meggie grinned cheekily at Rose. 'But you know what would help in the meantime?'

Rose laughed. 'What Meggie? What would help?'

'Coffee. It's morning, so coffee would help.' Meggie giggled. 'But around four o'clock this afternoon, wine will be the answer!'

Rose laughed and threw her arms around Meggie. 'I love you! Give me ten minutes and we'll head into town. My friend Deb owns the best coffee shop.'

4

Max hesitated at the door to the clinic. He looked down at Tommy. 'Ready mate?'

Tommy grinned at his father. 'I'll be so polite and quiet, you won't recognise me Dad.'

Max chuckled and shook his head. 'You're a good kid Tommy. Just be yourself.' Hiding his own nervousness, he pushed open the door and a little bell tinkled. Stepping inside, he closed the door. Max looked around the clinic waiting room, it was empty. He looked toward the reception counter. Unattended. He cleared his throat loudly.

A door beyond reception opened and a tall man stepped out, striding toward them. He had a friendly smile and looked from Max to Tommy and back to Max. His face showed nothing more than pleased curiosity.

'Angus Hamilton. You must be Max.' He held his hand out, shaking Max's hand firmly. Then he looked at Tommy, with an eyebrow raised. 'And you must be Max's assistant.'

Before Max could speak, Tommy held his small hand out to shake with Angus. 'I'm Tommy. I'm going to be a vet too when I grow up, like Dad.'

'Excellent.' Angus grinned at Max. 'Two for the price of one.' He paused for a moment. 'This is the waiting room, and reception is over there. Melanie is our full-time receptionist and Vet Nurse, but we close at three on weekdays unless there's an emergency. I attend to the large animal work in the afternoons.' Angus turned the sign on the front door to 'closed.'

Max looked around. The waiting room and reception area was clean and more modern than he expected. He nodded to Angus before turning to speak to Tommy. 'You can wait here Tommy, while I see the rest of the clinic with Angus.' Tommy slid his backpack off and sat in the nearest chair.

'Well Max, if Tommy is going to be here with you for the three months, he should come on the tour too.' Angus looked questioningly at Max.

Taking a breath, Max chided himself for not explaining his situation to Angus before he came. He badly wanted this to work out. He and Tommy need the change, the shift from their usual routines.

Quite firmly, but quietly, Max responded. 'He will be with me Mr Hamilton.' He paused as he watched Tommy stand up, not bothering to hide his eagerness. 'It's just the two of us. Now.'

Angus said okay, not asking for an explanation and Max felt relief wash over him. They followed Angus through to the surgery and operating theatre, then out through a back door to a newer building, a small animal hospital. There were two dogs in residence, one bandaged around his front leg, sitting quietly and another sleeping in an enclosure.

'What happened to these dogs Mr Hamilton?' Tommy knelt in front of the sleeping dog, who opened an eye and wagged his tail slowly.

'Call me Angus, Tommy.' Angus crouched down beside the boy, opening the door of the enclosure. He reached in and gave the dog a gentle pat. 'Shadow was bitten by a snake yesterday. A king brown. He's had anti-venom, but it took a while to work. We're keeping him under observation for another night.' He turned to the other dog. 'This one fell off the back of a tractor. Broke his leg. He'll go home tomorrow too.'

Standing up, Angus turned to Max. 'There are days when we don't have any animals overnight, but sometimes there are several. As I mentioned on the phone, there is a flat attached, I sleep in here when I have an animal that needs intensive care. But its available for you, and Tommy, as part of our arrangement. I'll take you through to it.' Angus opened a plastic container, offering it to Tommy. 'You can give the dogs a bit of dry food each if you like.'

Tommy took a handful, tipped half into his lap then reached out to Shadow, holding the rest of the food in his open hand. Shadow gently nibbled the food, then licked Tommy's hand thoroughly. Tommy crooned gently to the dog, giving him a pat before turning to the next one.

Angus stepped away and Max followed. Tommy was happily patting the dogs, speaking softly to them while they ate.

Max looked Angus in the eye. 'I didn't mention Tommy. I,

we, really need the change. He's a good kid, he's used to animals and he's good at keeping himself busy when I'm working.' Max exhaled, waiting for Angus to respond.

'It's all good Max. I can see Tommy is a great kid. I have no problem at all.' Angus eye-balled Max. They were a similar height. 'I can talk to you about school options too. Melanie's daughter starts Grade Four at Barrington when school returns in a couple of weeks. What year is Tommy in?'

Max's relief was palpable, he was sure Angus was aware of it too. 'He's going into Grade Four too. Should be Grade Three, he's eight, but he started early. Needed the stimulation.' He knew his pride was showing, but Tommy was bright. It was great to see him so happy and relaxed today, but perhaps he was simply reflecting Max's own mood.

With the dogs settled, Angus took Max and Tommy through to the apartment. It was little more than an oversize motel room, but had a kitchenette, bathroom, lounge area with television on the wall and a large bed. Tommy had been sleeping with Max for months, so it would do. For now. If the job turned into something more permanent, Max would rent a bigger place.

The men chatted about the work, the patients, the schedule and ended the meeting with a handshake.

'Are you driving back to Newcastle today Max?' Angus walked out through the front door with them, locking it as he went.

Max looked at his watch. 'Yes, we'll get back before dark if we go now. We've got a bit to organise so I'm ready to start on Monday next. Is it okay if we arrive next Saturday, to settle in?'

'Sure. Give me a call when you're close, I'll meet you here.' Angus shook hands again with Max, then Tommy. Max was proud of the way his boy looked up at Angus as they shook hands.

'I'll get the paperwork to you by email on Monday. Any questions, give me a call on the mobile. Any tricky questions and you might be better to call Melanie on the main phone, she's got all the admin information.' Angus grinned.

Ten minutes later they were driving out of town, heading to Newcastle.

'It went well, didn't it Dad?' Tommy was still in a state of happy excitement.

Max glanced at Tommy. 'It did mate. It went really well. I like Angus Hamilton, and I think his Vet practice is thriving. I'm going to do such a great job, that at the end of three months he'll want to keep me. Keep us.'

'You're a great Vet Dad. The best. Of course he'll want us to stay.'

Max turned the radio up, it was the local station playing country music. They sang along with Kasey Chambers' *Am I not Pretty Enough*, laughing loudly at each other. As he drove, the tightness in his chest loosened another notch.

5

A week in Barrington and Meggie already knew a bunch of locals by name. She'd driven into town in Rose's bright red Jeep, with a list of jobs to do and groceries to fetch. With only six weeks to the wedding, Meggie was employing all her event management skills.

Sipping on her second chai latte, Meggie scrolled through the spreadsheet on her iPad. Rose and Angus were getting married at Barrington Homestead with a core group of family and friends in attendance, so it wasn't a big wedding. She'd convinced them to get a marquee for the backyard for the dinner and dancing, leaving the homestead kitchen for the caterers and the wide verandas for pre-dinner drinks and canapes. The ceremony would be simple, conducted by a civil celebrant near the front steps. It was perfect, really. Meggie sighed. It was *her* perfect wedding, and she wondered, for a moment, if she had pushed her wedding concept a little too hard. But Rose had been happy to leave it to Meggie.

'Hey Meggie, how are the plans coming along?' Debbie slid into the seat across from her, a coffee in her hand.

'I was thinking how simple and easy this one is. I'm so used to big. Not just big. Huge. Monstrous weddings in Napa.' Meggie made a face at Debbie. 'And not only the weddings. The brides. Monsters, all of them!'

'Ha! I've heard stories about bridezillas. But you won't get that here. Not with Rose.' Debbie sipped her coffee, then screwed up her nose, making Meggie smile. 'Rose isn't a girlie girl. Her only real wish is to be married at the homestead, with as little fuss as possible.'

'There will be fuss.' Meggie's eyes twinkled. 'Not much, but enough. I want this to be beautiful and memorable. For Rose, Angus and all of us on the day. But I understand her wish for simplicity, so that's what we'll have. Simple elegance. Maybe a little bit traditional too, in keeping with the setting.'

'Oooh, sounds like you have some surprises up your sleeve Meggie. Let me know if you need a hand.' Debbie finished her coffee and glanced at the counter. The mid-morning rush was beginning.

'We still need to sort out your matron-of-honour outfit Debbie. The bridal store in Newcastle is sending the wedding gown up next week. We'll have a fitting and consider a style that works with it for you.' Meggie started to rise. 'I've got some ideas. We'll talk.'

'Sure. Let me know when. My mother-in-law said she'd have little Charlie for an afternoon, she's watching Woz anyway, so we can sort the dress out.' Debbie turned.

'Woz?' Meggie was laughing. 'I'd forgotten how much we shorten names here. What's your little boy's name?'

'Warwick. But he'll get Woz once he starts school. We're getting him used to it.' Debbie grinned, then sped toward the counter where a small group were waiting.

Laughing to herself, Meggie packed her iPad and notebook into her satchel. She'd only met Debbie a week ago and could see how close she was to Rose. Both confident, generous women, they had immediately pulled Meggie into their circle, including her without forethought. Walking toward the Vet Clinic, Meggie looked up and down the street. She liked this little town. While she knew she'd get a job in the city with her qualifications and experience, she wondered if she could find a job here, in Barrington.

Accommodation was also on Meggie's mind. Most of the wedding guests were local, so that wasn't her problem. Meggie and Angus's mum Helen and new partner Barry were arriving in two weeks, staying through the wedding and honeymoon. They were going to wrangle little Charlie for three weeks while Rose and Angus enjoyed their honeymoon. Meggie chuckled. While she knew they'd been frequent visitors to Barrington Homestead since Charlie was born, she wondered how they'd manage for a full three weeks. Charlie's adorable, but a handful. But they would need to stay at the house and the guest wing that Meggie was currently occupying was the logical place. There was a guest room in the main house, that Rose and Angus suggested she move into, but she had in mind something more permanent. Something of her own.

Pushing open the door of the Vet Clinic, Meggie glanced around. Only two patients waiting.

'Hi Meggie.' Melanie, the Vet Nurse, called out and gestured her to the reception area with a smile. 'Angus won't be long, only has a couple of patients, then we'll close for lunch for an hour.'

'Hi Melanie. Thank you.' Meggie was about to take a seat and wait for Angus, but she turned back to Melanie. 'You're a long-time local Melanie?'

'Sure am. Grew up here. Can I help with something?'

'Yes please. There's a few real estate agents in the main street, can you recommend who might best provide some advice? On accommodation.' Meggie nibbled her lip.

'If it's for wedding guests, you might be better speaking to the local tourism officer. I can give you Wendy's number.' Melanie picked up a pen and post-it note.

'Well. Not really for guests. Our mum and step-dad are coming for an extended stay, and I want to give them the guest suite at the homestead. I thought I might try and find something in town for myself.'

'Oh, of course. It's a pity the locum will be using the flat here at the clinic, which might have done for a couple of months. He arrives tomorrow.' Melanie, picked up a business card from her desk, handing it across to Meggie. 'Drop into Evans Real Estate, it's a few doors further down the street.' She pointed to the name on the card. 'Ben Evans, er junior, is my husband. He'll look after you. If he's not in, Harriet Russell will sort you out.'

'Your husband? Perfect, I'll go there right now. Can you tell Angus I'll come back at noon, maybe we can have lunch together?' Meggie thanked Melanie with a nod and moved toward the door.

'No problem, I'll let him know. Good luck.'

* * *

PUSHING OPEN THE DOOR OF EVANS REAL ESTATE, MEGGIE glanced in. A blonde woman about her own age was speaking on the phone at a desk to one side. There was a beautiful sign on the wall behind her stating 'Barrington – A Place to Start Over.' The words resonated with Meggie. That's exactly what she hoped to do. Start over. The woman was welcoming and gestured towards a chair in front of her desk, so Meggie sat down.

Putting the phone down, the woman walked around the desk, hand out to shake Meggie's. 'Hi, I'm Harriet, thanks for coming in.' While shaking Meggie's hand, she looked up at her for a moment, then grinned broadly. 'You must be Meggie! I can see your likeness to Angus, and a bit to your mum too. Tall people, all of you!'

'Nice to meet you Harriet.' Meggie relaxed. 'This is a small town thing, isn't it? Where everyone knows everyone? I bet you're a generational local like Rose, Debbie and Melanie.'

'Ha, not so much! Actually, I moved here a bit more than a year ago from Sydney and I absolutely love it!' Harriet radiated warmth and Meggie felt drawn to her. 'But you're returning from quite a few years in California, if I have my facts right, so Barrington must seem really small after that.'

'It's different, of course. But in a good way. I already know a bunch of people and the café down the street makes my favourite coffee before I finish ordering and I've only been here a week!' Meggie knew she sounded excited, but she had such a good feeling about the place.

'Debbie has that place running so well, it's a real draw-card for the town. I don't know how she does it with a one-year-old, but she has a great team, and her mum and mother-in-law are local and help with little Warwick.'

'The coffee there is brilliant. Better than the States, actually. Australians are much snobbier about their coffee than almost any other place I've been.' Meggie laughed out loud at the thought, 'good barista-made coffee in Australia has definitely become a *thing*, even in small towns.'

Chuckling with her, Harriet added, 'The coffee is good and you're right, we expect that now, even in small towns. And I'm so glad to finally meet you, Angus has been speaking of you a lot since you said you'd return for the wedding.'

'It's really nice to meet you too, Harriet.' Meggie pulled out the business card Melanie had given her. 'Melanie said her husband Ben owns the business. I'm actually looking for some real estate advice.'

'That's great. Ben's out with clients but perhaps I can help.' Harriet raised her eyebrows.

Meggie pointed at the sign on the wall. 'That's what I'm looking for. A place to start over.' She took a breath. 'I really haven't discussed it with Angus and Rose in any detail, but I've decided not to return to the United States. If I can find work and a place of my own, I think I'd like to stay here.'

6

'It's not big mate, but we'll be cosy here.' Max looked around the apartment. Their bags were in a pile on the floor, the space looked much smaller than he remembered. Taking another look at the kitchenette area, Max noted the fridge was little more than a bar fridge and the cooking appliances consisted of a microwave, toaster and kettle. He frowned. It was enough for breakfasts and lunches but perhaps an air fryer would help for some dinners. He'd left everything in their house in Newcastle, as he'd rented it out for the three months. He brightened. There was the café and a couple of pubs for dinners, they'd be fine. Tommy wasn't a fussy eater.

He smiled. Tommy was already setting up his gaming console. The television on the wall was at least a late model one. He'd also brought a big plastic tub of Lego, but Max knew that Tommy would prefer hanging out with him in the clinic before and after school to help look after patients in the animal hospital. The area was full of places to bushwalk, mountain bike and canoe and Max thought they'd have a crack at those on his days off.

Glancing at his watch, he ruffled Tommy's hair. 'Want to have lunch at the café? Then we can buy a few groceries.'

Tommy stood up quickly. 'Sure Dad, I'm starving.'

They went out through the back, rather than walk through the clinic, which was closed. Their car was parked at the rear, Angus had met them when they arrived and directed them to the rear entrance, where he'd walked through and given them the keys to the apartment and clinic. He'd invited them out to his home for dinner, but Max had politely declined, saying he wanted to get settled in. Angus had said they'd have plenty of opportunities during the coming weeks.

As they walked down a side lane back to the main street, Tommy was asking questions about school. He was starting on Monday and seemed curious rather than anxious. Max was relieved. He'd seen a big change in his son since their trip to Barrington the week before. He felt it too. A fresh start, a different environment. It was what they needed.

The café was quiet, lunch time almost over. Debbie, from last week wasn't there but the girl that served them was friendly and they didn't wait long for their sandwiches. Tommy's chatter stopped the moment the food arrived, and with eyebrows raised in amazement Max watched him devour his sandwich and milkshake. After months of moping and a lack of interest in food, it was heartening to see Tommy so animated. Max enjoyed his sandwich and coffee too and he knew the change in Tommy was a reflection of his own mood, returning slowly to a sense of normality.

They filled the rest of the weekend in setting themselves up in the apartment and exploring some of the walking trails close to town. They kicked a football around in the park on Sunday afternoon, and then took a walk around the Barrington School grounds, to familiarise Tommy before the next day.

'What do you think Tommy. It's a bit different from Newcastle Grammar.' There were only a few buildings, three of them classrooms and one a library and maybe admin space. Max had spoken to the Principal during the week, they were happy to have Tommy and would put him in a Year 3 & 4 composite class. Tommy had the requisite grey shorts, blue shirt and black shoes for day one and Max would buy a couple of the school sports tee shirts for other days.

'It's really small isn't it Dad? But it has a tennis court over there, and a footy oval.' Tommy pointed and Max noted how neat the sports fields were. In a small town like this there was likely a parent working bee for stuff like that. He'd check into it, put his name down to help out. He really wanted to get to know the people here, and the parents of Tommy's classmates would be a good start.

'It's small, but I've heard that small schools are better. Less kids in class, friendlier.' He glanced down at his son as they walked back to the car. 'Are you worried about it?'

'Nah. I'm not worried about it. But I'm hoping I'll make some friends.' Max opened the car door and waited while Tommy settled himself with the seatbelt on.

'You'll make friends Tommy. Some of the kids will be farm kids. You might be invited to their farms where they'll have dogs, cattle, horses and all sorts of chores to do.'

'That'd be cool. I'd really like to ride a horse.' He bounced in his seat. 'That would be the best. A new friend with a farm, and horses!'

Max chuckled to himself as they drove back to the clinic. Then he frowned. Tommy wouldn't be able to reciprocate with a sleepover, they only had one bed. If it seemed to be working out in the first few weeks, he'd look at renting something bigger. He glanced across at Tommy and a sob caught in his chest. The shape of his face, his delicate ear, so much like his mother. The sight caught him unawares, his fingers tightened on the steering wheel.

With some sort of weird sixth sense, Tommy knew. He spoke quietly. 'Are you thinking about Mum?'

Max let out the breath he didn't realise he was holding. He looked sadly at Tommy. 'Yep. I am. I think about her a lot. But Tommy?'

'Yes Dad?'

'Being here. In Barrington. It's better than being at home isn't it? A fresh start?' Max watched the emotions play across his son's face.

'I like it here Dad. We'll never forget Mum. But somehow, it's easier being here, away from our house. Away from everything. I think we can be happy here Dad.'

Max was barely able to speak. He swallowed, then grinned at Tommy. 'I think we can be happy here too. Of course we'll never forget Mum but thinking about her seems to hurt less here.'

Tommy wiped the back of his hand across his eyes. Seeing that small gesture nearly undid Max. 'I love you Dad.'

'Love you too, son.' They looked at each other then, as

they pulled up at the back of the clinic. Both with tears in their eyes. Without warning Tommy laughed. The sound was infectious. Max found himself laughing too. 'What?' he said. But Tommy couldn't answer, he laughed even harder. They opened the car doors and Max found himself bent over at the waist, laughing. Really laughing. He didn't know why, but it felt good.

Tommy came around the car and threw his arms around Max, tears of laughter running down his face. 'We're turning into a couple of sooks Dad. We're in the country now. We need to man up!' This brought on another bout of laughter, and they walked inside, Max with his arm around Tommy's slight shoulders. The moment had been good for them. There was something about this little town, it was working its magic on them. Max felt lighter. Laughing was good, natural. And he didn't feel guilty about having a happy moment.

7

M eggie put her wine glass down. 'I'd forgotten how good Australian wine is. Everyone raves about Napa Valley vintages, but honestly, this is better than anything I tasted over there.' She picked up the bottle and looked at the label. 'Tyrrells. Semillon. Of course. One of the first dozen winemakers in Australia. Hunter Valley, established in the eighteen fifties.'

Rose snorted. 'Oh you know your wines. I just drink what I like, and this one goes perfectly with my Thai beef salad.'

Meggie grinned at Angus as he topped up their glasses. 'When I left you were purely a beer man Gus. Did Rose civilise your taste buds?'

'Thank you very much Megs. I was always civilised. Sophisticated even. But you were too young to notice.' He picked up his glass, little finger sticking out and took a delicate sip.

'Oh stop Angus!' Rose turned to Meggie, laughing. 'He

had two quick beers when he came home, so he's happy to share a wine now. He's trying to impress you.'

Meggie sat back, watching Angus and Rose banter back and forth. Little Charlie was asleep and with the evening still warm they had decided on a late dinner. She wanted to tell them about giving up her suite and moving out before the wedding but hadn't found the right moment. She knew Rose was enjoying her company and as well as planning the wedding, Meggie had been able to look after Charlie most afternoons and Rose was getting some writing done. She was an accomplished author and Meggie admired her for it, although she had no idea how she found time most days.

'Did Max arrive today? Do you think he'll be keen to stay longer than three months?' Rose asked as she passed the salad to Angus.

Meggie watched as Angus served himself. She knew that look. Angus was thinking before he spoke. She glanced at Rose, and almost laughed. Rose knew that look too.

'He did arrive on time. They did.' Angus passed the salad back to Rose and chewed thoughtfully on a mouthful.

'They?' What do you mean *they*? I thought he was on his own? You didn't say anything about a partner. Wife?' Rose fired her questions off in quick succession and Meggie could see that Angus was drawing it out, but she was curious too.

'I know. He has a pet. A dog. Or a fish. Maybe a turtle.' Meggie giggled as she took a bite of salad. It was really good. Fresh. Crisp. A little spicy. It suited the wine perfectly.

'No. Not a pet. He has a Tommy.' Angus was enjoying this. Meggie glanced at Rose. She had her thinking face on.

Rose spoke up. 'I know. Boyfriend. Tommy is his boyfriend.'

Angus shook his head. 'Give in?'

Meggie elbowed him. 'We're not five! Tell us!'

'Tommy is his eight-year-old son.' Angus sipped his wine. Meggie and Rose looked at each in surprise.

'His son? Just the two of them? Did he even ask you about this? Where's the mother?' Rose was drumming the table with her fingertips.

'I knew. He brought Tommy with him last week. He's a nice kid, wants to be a vet too. He was really good with the two dogs in hospital.' Angus leaned forward. 'Honestly? He didn't tell me why. But I can see they've been through something. I think they're grieving. I also think he's taken this job to give them a fresh start, or a change of scenery at least. Perhaps somewhere the memories aren't as strong.'

'Oh. Oh that's sad.' Meggie and Rose looked at each other.

'Why didn't you invite them for dinner?' Rose now glared at Angus. 'I could have cooked something suitable for all of us.' Meggie agreed.

'I did. He declined. I don't think he's ready.' Angus reached for the wine and poured the last of it into the girls' glasses. 'He was wound up I think, waiting for questions. I didn't give him any and he relaxed.' He looked carefully at his wife and sister. 'So don't come in on Monday and interrogate him. He'll tell us when he's ready and I'll invite him for dinner again next week. Let them settle in. He has Tommy booked into school on Monday, so I'm hoping that's a sign he's thinking more long term. My gut feeling is he's a good Vet and I can already see he's a good dad.'

'The flat at the clinic isn't very big. It only has one bed and not much of a kitchen at all.' Rose began clearing the table.

Angus stood to help her. 'I know that Rose. But let them settle. I'm sure Max knows what he's doing.' She sighed, said yes.

Meggie stood, her moment to discuss her own situation seemed to have passed. She'd had a good talk with Harriet the day before and was going to look at a two bedroom rental on Monday. It was across the road from the Vet Clinic, the top floor of the Post Office. It used to be the residence for the Postmaster General, back in the day, but Australia Post had been renting it out, often to staff, for decades. While Meggie didn't need two bedrooms, it was loads cheaper than a one bedroom in the city. She'd also spoken to Harriet about buying a second-hand car. She said she knew of one that might be in the right price range.

Carrying the last dishes through to the kitchen, Rose was already washing up and Angus drying. Meggie said a quick thank you for dinner and goodnight and left them to it. Back in her room, she sat on the bed for a moment, not sure if she wanted to have a good cry, or long bath. She decided on the bath. Her decision to move on from her old life, old situation, was good. She'd find her way here. There were good people around her and the warmth she received from Angus and Rose cemented that decision. Having family around, and friends, was pure gold.

8

'Are you ready mate? Your first day at Barrington School?' Max unbuckled his seatbelt, they were parked with several others in front of the school.

'Yep.' Tommy looked excited and nervous at the same time.

There were several parents milling around the front gate, some with smaller children in oversize uniforms. One little girl was crying in her father's arms and Max watched as an older child came from inside the school grounds and spoke to them. After a few moments the father put his child down, her tears had stopped, and she took the older girl's hand and allowed herself to be led inside the schoolyard.

About to step out of the car, Max was startled by a tap on his window. A cheerful-looking blonde woman was standing there. Tommy was already scrambling out of the car on the other side, his backpack slung over one shoulder.

Opening the door, Max stepped out. 'Hello.' Tommy came

around the car and stood beside him, looking curiously at the woman.

'You must be Max. And Tommy. I'm Melanie, from the clinic. Angus told me to watch out for you today and I know everyone else here, so it was easy to find you.' She looked toward the school gate. 'Tiff! Tiffany! Come and say hello.'

'Oh hi Melanie, nice to meet you.' Tommy was fidgeting, and Max knew it was a sign of nerves. Two girls, about Tommy's age, ran up. Both fair, one was petite and obviously Melanie's daughter. Her friend was taller, her hair blonde and curly.

'Tommy, this is my daughter Tiffany and her friend Billie. I think they are in your grade.' Melanie nudged her daughter forward a little.

The other girl, Billie, gestured to Tommy. 'Come on, we'll show you our classroom.' Tommy looked from Max to Billie and Tiffany. They were starting to turn toward the school gate. He hesitated. Billie stepped back, waiting. 'I started here last year, it's a great school. Much better than my old one in Sydney. Come on.' Tommy took a step toward the girls, then turned to Max. 'Seeya Dad. Have a good day.' Then he was running with the girls, into the school grounds.

Max let out a sigh, then turned back to Melanie. 'Thank you Melanie. The girls will break the ice for him.' He chuckled. 'But there might be a conversation tonight about girls as he hasn't been friends with any before. They're like a whole other species to Tommy.'

Melanie chuckled. 'I hear you, but it's a funny thing with small schools. They seem to generally all play together. They kinda have to, to make up teams for any sports and it translates back into the classroom.' They walked back to their cars together.

Melanie stopped for a moment. 'I'm sure you'll want to pick up Tommy today, and maybe all this week. But I was thinking that once he's settled, I can pick him up when I get Tiff and he can hang out with us some afternoons. Billie comes home with us sometimes too, but she lives on a farm further out and often gets the bus.'

Max looked away for a moment. Melanie's words brought a lump to his throat. He'd been worried about juggling Tommy and work in the afternoons, especially if he had to go out to a property. He'd expected to take him everywhere he went. To find some help, some support, on their first day really touched him. He looked back at Melanie. 'Thank you. Thank you very much. I'd really like that, and I hope we can return the favour and help out with Tiffany too.'

'Of course. That's how we operate here.' Melanie smiled over her shoulder as she walked to her car. 'See you in the clinic shortly.' Max waved and opened his car door.

'Oh Max?'

'Yes.'

'How do you like your coffee? I'm picking one up for all of us this morning. You know, a welcome to the business thing.'

Max grinned. 'I never say no to coffee. Americano please.'

Melanie gave a thumbs up and got into her car. Max waited while she backed out, then he pulled out and drove into the clinic. He sang along to the local radio station all the way.

* * *

THE MORNING PASSED QUICKLY. MAX WORKED ALONGSIDE ANGUS in the clinic, seeing to a variety of patients. This was where he felt most comfortable. Small animal clinic. While the patients and ailments were largely familiar, the clients were quite different. Polite, friendly, grateful. Sure, he had a lot of pleasant clients at the Newcastle practice, but there were also many who were rushed, ill-mannered, neurotic and difficult.

'That's it for the morning Max.' Angus stretched. 'We need to get some lunch then we're off to preg-test heifers out at Drum Murray's property. He has a mare in foal too, so we'll check her while we're there.'

'Great. You've really got a busy practice here Angus, I heard Melanie rescheduling some for tomorrow morning that we couldn't fit in.' Max washed up at the sink in the surgery. Their last patient, a cattle dog, had required stitches in her side after an incident with a barb-wire fence.

'I can see you're at home in the clinic already. No need for us to work together here all the time.' Angus chuckled. 'You hardly need supervision.' He moved over to the sink as Max finished, saying over his shoulder, 'I'd like to take you to a few of the properties where we do most of our big animal work, horses and cattle mainly. A few sheep, some goats and there's an alpaca farm too. Do you want to grab lunch together at the café? I've already got some ideas on how best to move forward.'

'Lunch would be great. Thanks Angus.' They walked out to reception together, Angus speaking briefly to Melanie before they left the clinic.

'Does Melanie take a lunch break?' Max noted he and Angus were a similar height and build, although Max knew he was a few years older.

'Mel likes to eat at her desk, that way she can finish at three to pick Tiff up from school.' Angus glanced at Max. 'She's a really good vet nurse, practically runs the business side for me too.' He hesitated. 'She will help out with Tommy. Pick him up and keep him after school. If you need it, that is.'

'She offered this morning, at school. Introduced Tommy to her daughter and a friend.' Max hesitated. 'I'm grateful.' Angus said 'good,' as if it was no big deal.

They sat at an outside table. Max glanced at the menu then at Angus. 'What's good? I'm starving. Must be the country air.'

'It's a burger for me. Chips and salad. Can't go wrong.' Angus hadn't even looked at the menu. Max stood. 'I'll order for us.' Before Angus could respond Max was at the counter chatting with Debbie.

He returned with cutlery and napkins. 'Debbie said you usually have an iced coffee at lunchtime, so I've ordered that too.'

'Thanks Max. You don't have to buy lunch for me.' Angus grinned. 'But it's gonna taste better 'cos I didn't pay.' He threw his head back and laughed and Max joined him.

'There is something I need to talk to you about Angus. Now might be a good time.' Max spoke quietly.

'Go ahead mate.' Angus focussed on Max, nodding encouragement.

'Tommy and me. We're on our own.' Max paused, looked down for a moment, then back at Angus. 'My wife, Liliana, was killed in a car accident almost a year ago.' He paused as their drinks were delivered to the table.

'Mate, you don't have to explain anything. I realised there was a reason you were here, and not because you have Tommy with you. A change, or a fresh start. It's all good with me. I'm already confident you can take care of the clinic while I'm away.'

'You're right. We need the change. So badly that I didn't tell you our situation, or about Tommy. I hoped you'd be okay with it.' Max took a sip of his drink, then looked Angus in the eye. 'Thank you.'

Their burgers came and they tucked in with gusto. 'And about Melanie. Nice lady. I'm hoping we can work together with the kids a bit, share the drop-offs and pick-ups. After-noons especially when I'm away from the clinic.' Max grinned. 'Although Tommy would give his eye teeth to come out to the properties, especially equine work. He's horse-mad.'

'We've got horses. Well, Rose has. Bring him out next weekend, we'll have a barbecue. Rose can introduce him to her horses.' Angus put his cutlery down, he'd eaten about half of the burger. 'This calls for a more aggressive approach.' He picked the remains of the burger up in his hands and took a large bite. Max laughed. The relief he felt at finally telling Angus lightened his mood, his whole being.

9

Meggie followed Harriet upstairs to the post office apartment. The wide staircase was made of solid timber and the treads were old and worn, although the exterior of the building was sandstone and as solid as the day it was built, around nineteen hundred. They came to a small landing, also timber, the boards old and gnarly, but polished and clean. Harriet opened the door to the apartment and Meggie stepped into an enormous open living room. It may have been two rooms at one stage, there was a decorative timber arch high in the centre of the room and large windows, not quite floor to ceiling, along the street-facing side.

The kitchen ran along the wall at one end of the big room and Harriet took Meggie through to a smaller area, now a butler's pantry that also enclosed a washer and dryer.

'So gorgeous! I'm really surprised it hasn't been used as holiday accommodation.' Meggie turned around in the small room. 'What would this little room have been used for, back in the day?'

'Probably a broom closet or cleaning room. There are back stairs right out there, down the exterior of the building into the laneway. Needed to meet fire emergency guidelines, but I'd say they used it for access to the backyard. They would have had a clothesline and kitchen garden out there. And an outside toilet and laundry.' Harriet walked back into the main living area.

'There are two bedrooms, they wrap around the other side of the building as the staircase really comes right up through the middle.' Meggie followed Harriet through another door. The bedrooms were large with good size windows, and a bathroom sat between them. The apartment was furnished, some of it a bit dated, but solid enough. Meggie was entranced. She had no idea she could rent something like this in Barrington.

'I'll take it! When can I move in, it's perfect for me!' Meggie almost skipped back to the kitchen. It had a big fridge and a gas stove. She clapped her hands. And while it was quite warm upstairs today, she could see a large reverse cycle air-conditioner in the living area.

'As soon as we get the lease signed. I'll email it to Australia Post, but they're usually pretty quick. Come back down, we'll go to my office, it's cooler there.'

Meggie followed Harriet out into the street, then across the road to her office.

'Cold drink Meggie? I have some diet soda out in the kitchen.' Harriet raised a questioning brow.

'Thank you, yes please. I'm still not used to the heat, although it's only been a week.'

While Harriet brought the drinks through, Meggie placed her passport and other identification on the desk. She looked across at Harriet. 'I don't have any current rental references. My accommodation in Napa was provided by the company.'

'Not to worry. You've got identification and you have family locally. I'll referee you myself.' Harriet set about handing the lease documents across, indicating where Meggie should sign.

'I've made it for six months, but I'm sure we can extend it if you need.'

'Great! I'm serious, I'd like to stay here.' Meggie looked up, her hand poised to initial the next page.

'I know you're serious. But I am curious about your plans. You have the wedding to organise, but after that?' Harriet seemed genuinely interested, so Meggie took a deep breath.

'Well. It's a small town, I realise that. But it's so beautiful. It could be a good place for weddings and events, you know wedding and engagement tourism.' Meggie sat back, watching Harriet's reaction. She wasn't disappointed, Harriet leaned forward.

'Brilliant Meggie, bloody brilliant! We need your skills here. But you're thinking too narrowly.'

Meggie laughed. She was pumped. She wanted to discuss this with Rose and Angus but wasn't sure of their reaction. 'Too narrowly? How?'

'Think bigger. Bigger events. Australia Day. A festival here, showcasing local food, art, music. Great for tourism. Then reproduce that a few times a year. A winter festival. So many come here from the city for the snow. While we don't get it down here, it's where everyone starts before heading up to Barrington Tops when there's a fall. Spring. You could do something around weddings. Like a fair.' Harriet drew a breath and sat back.

'Really? I love these ideas. Getting paid as a wedding organiser is one thing, but how does it work when putting something together for the town, the community?' Meggie's mind was racing, but she was mindful it would be a business too. 'Community events are great, but they don't pay the organiser very much.'

'Funding Meggie. Grant funding. Council funding for tourism and small business. State funding. We could put a proposal together for a few main events each year and take it to Council, then the State. Sponsors too.' Harriet waved her hand around the office. 'Evans Real Estate would sponsor and there'd be others. You'd be bringing opportunity to the area, showcasing it.'

'Wow! Thanks Harriet. Great ideas.' Meggie paused. 'But they're your ideas, why would you give them to me?'

'It's an opportunity that's too big for me, and while I have some of the skills, I'm lacking in areas that you have an abundance of. Think about it. I'm happy to give you the ideas. Take them. Run with them.' She paused. 'But I'd also be happy to talk collaboration. Partnership perhaps. But no pressure.' Harriet scooped the lease up. 'First things first. Let's get you moved in across the street. I think you'll be good to go by the end of the week. When does your mother arrive?'

'Next weekend, so that's perfect. And we have a wedding dress fitting this week and I'm yet to organise Debbie's matron-of-honour dress. So a bit to do.' Meggie stood up. 'I'll talk it through with Angus and Rose too. Can I get back to you on the business thing?'

'Of course. No rush. I can't see anyone else jumping into the marketplace. Wait until after the wedding if you'd rather.' Harriet walked around her desk, but Meggie could see she was excited too.

'No.' Meggie spoke firmly.

Harriet seemed taken aback. 'No what?'

'No I won't wait. I'll talk it through with Angus and Rose and I'll do some research. I'll let you know my thoughts by the end of the week.' Meggie spoke in a rush, then breathed out. 'I'm really excited! I'm really-bloody-excited! No waiting Harriet. I need to work out the details, business structure options and budgets. But I'm in!'

Glancing at her watch, Meggie saw it was past lunchtime and wondered if Angus would have time for a chat. As she neared the Vet Clinic, she saw Angus walking toward her with another man. Max, the Locum Vet, she assumed. He was easily as tall as Angus and broader across the shoulders. She raised a hand in greeting as they neared her, now at the front door to the clinic.

'Hey Megs. Are you looking for me?' Angus looked pleased, then turned toward the other man. 'Max, this is my sister Meggie. Meggie. Max.'

Meggie looked up at him. 'Hi Max, nice to meet you.' He took her hand in his and she immediately noticed how big it was. She was a tall woman and secretly thought she had man-hands, but hers seemed almost delicate, and feminine, gripped in his giant paw. He mouthed a greeting, but she barely heard it, as she stared at their hands. Suddenly she realised he had relaxed his grip and her hand was still in his. Blushing, she drew it back quickly.

If Angus noticed, he didn't comment. Inwardly she thought that was more for Max's benefit than hers and it was likely he'd tease her later.

Meggie turned to Angus. 'I was wondering if you'd have time for lunch, but I can see you're on your way back from the café, so I guess that's a no.'

'Sorry Megs. We're heading out to do some preg-testing. Was there anything urgent you wanted to talk about?' As Angus spoke, Max nodded at Meggie, then entered the clinic, leaving her outside with Angus.

Shaking her head, Meggie answered. 'No. Not really. Well, yes, I want to talk to you. And Rose. But it's not urgent. I'll join you for dinner tonight, for a chat, if that's okay?'

'Of course. Work it out with Rose. I won't be late.' Angus reached for the door.

'Max. The new guy. How's he working out?' Meggie inclined her head toward the door.

'So far he's been great.' Angus pulled the door open. 'We'll chat tonight then, okay?'

10

Walking from the heat of the day into the clinic, Max put his right hand in his pocket. It had tingled in an unfamiliar way when he'd gripped Meggie's. He clenched it a couple of times, then spoke quietly to Melanie. 'Any messages?'

'No. It's been quiet. Drum Murray called to say he has the heifers yarded, so you can head out there when Angus is ready.' Melanie walked to the copy machine as she spoke, then turned back to Max. 'You might need to take two vehicles out there if you want to be on time for Tommy this afternoon. Or I can pick him up when I get Tiff and drop him back later.'

'Thanks Melanie. I'm not sure. It's his first day and it's hard to know if it's been a good one.' As Max spoke, Angus walked through to reception.

'Was Billie at school this morning?' Angus directed this to Melanie.

'Yes, of course! She and Tiff took Tommy into class together.' Melanie turned to Max. 'Billie is Drum Murray's daughter. She'll go home on the bus or perhaps Harriet is picking her up. That's Drum's fiancée. I'll give Harri a call.' She was already dialling before Max had time to really follow the conversation.

Angus nudged Max. 'Let the girls work it out. Tommy can come out there with Billie and watch us finish the testing. Do you think he'd like that?'

Max relaxed. His shoulders had been tense, but he could see how hard they were trying to ensure Tommy was included. When he thought about it, he knew no matter what sort of day Tommy had, he'd still rather come and do 'vet stuff' than homework. 'Thanks Melanie. If you can work it out with, Harri is it?' Melanie nodded. 'If you can work it out with Harri, then Tommy will be happy knowing he's coming to 'work,' so thank you, that's perfect.'

Leaving the clinic in the Vet vehicle, Angus pointed out a few landmarks on the way to the Murray property, including the river and places to kayak and swim. Max leaned forward in his seat to get a better look. So many outdoor activities in this region.

Angus interrupted his thoughts, 'Tommy will be in good hands with Harriet. She came here little more than a year ago, runs a business within the Evans Real Estate agency.' He pointed to a cottage set back from the road, lovely gardens in the front yard. 'That's Bellbird Cottage. Harriet owns it. She's also Drum Murray's nearest neighbour.' Angus paused for a moment. 'Drum's divorced, his little girl Billie is with him full time. Harri's been great for both of them.' He glanced at Max.

'I don't know the personal details of all my clients, and probably wouldn't fill you in if I did. But Drum's a mate, you'll like him.'

Max thought about Angus' words. He wanted to get along with clients, and he appreciated the extra information provided by Angus. If Drum was a mate, Max wanted to make sure he looked after him. And if Tommy settled at school, he was really keen to make this a permanent move. They could sell the Newcastle house. He brought himself back to the present as they pulled up at a large shed, and cattle yards. Max could see at a glance it was a good operation, and a big property.

Angus made quick introductions and they started working. While Max hadn't done a lot of cattle work, he'd done enough to keep them moving into the holding pen for the test. They had more than sixty to run through. Angus did the first thirty while Max and Drum moved the cattle in, then out after the test. Max took over for the second half and found it easy going. The cattle were used to being handled and the facilities modern, making their job quicker than he'd expected.

They only had a few left when a little red car pulled up by the fence. Max didn't have time to do more than acknowledge Tommy had stepped out of the car with a woman and the little girl he'd met that morning, Billie. From the corner of his eye he could see Tommy sitting on the top rail of the fence.

'That's it Max, last one's through!' Angus called out from the other side of the fence.

'Right.' Max started packing their equipment up, then

walked out through the gate to stack it by the car. He found a tap on the side of the yards and turned it on, washing his hands and arms. Angus appeared beside him.

'Drum has a mare in foal, we're going to have a quick look at her before we go. The children have gone through to the stables with Drum.' Angus grinned. 'Your Tommy was practically jogging on the spot and Billie was giving him a lecture on being calm around the mare when they get there.' Max chuckled.

'Tommy's keen. And horse mad. But he knows to be calm around animals, so he'll be okay.'

They walked to the stables and Max marvelled at how comfortable he felt with Angus. And while he'd not spoken much to Drum, he could see the men were cut from the same cloth.

Inside the stable the mare was tethered in a large enclosure, her nose in a feedbag. Tommy came to stand quietly beside Max as they all looked at the mare for a moment.

'Hey Dad.' Max looked down. Tommy was grinning, his eyes shining, as he looked up at him.

Max ruffled his hair. 'Good day?'

'The best.' That was enough for Max, they could talk later. He stepped into the stall with Angus.

Billie and Tommy hung over the gate, watching. They didn't speak much, until Max heard Tommy ask her if she had a horse. 'Oh sure. Chippy and Lady are my favourites. Wanna come and see them?'

Max glanced up, checking with Drum.

'They're in the paddock right here, all good.' Drum turned

to his daughter. 'You and Tommy can take a bit of hay out to the feed bin for the horses, but don't go inside their paddock, you've still got your uniforms on.'

The kids disappeared and Max and Angus got on with checking the mare. Satisfied she, and the foal she carried, were in good health, they stepped outside the pen.

'A nice type of horse Drum. What's her breeding? Stock-horse? A bit of Arabian blood?' Max inclined his head toward the mare.

'She is a beauty. I bought her from Rose Gordon, her grandfather bred her from his old stallion, Topper. You're right, stock horse-Arabian cross. Rose broke her in, but she hasn't been ridden much. The foal is by my stallion, Jack. She's for Harriet to ride once she's foaled.' Drum folded his arms across his chest. Max thought he looked pleased with himself.

'Do you have time to come up to the house for a cuppa or a cold one?' Drum led them outside. Max could see two horses eating from the feed bin, but no sign of Billie and Tommy.

'We'll come up Drum.' Angus nudged Max. 'That's where your son will be.'

Drum laughed. 'Billie and Harri baked a carrot cake last night. They wanted to welcome the new vet. Tommy is a bonus.'

'What about me?' Angus tried to look miffed, 'I'm the old vet and I don't get baked goods when I come here.' He shook his head. 'Well, not every time anyway.'

They walked to the homestead together, chatting generally about cattle, horses, dogs and the weather. Max relaxed, enjoying the easy conversation. If Tommy asked how his day was later he'd give the same answer. The best.

11

Little Charlie was finally down for the night and Meggie, Rose and Angus had moved to the back veranda, relaxing in the slightly cooler evening air.

'How was Max today Angus?' Rose passed a platter of cheese and olives across to him. Meggie shot a quick look at Angus, keen to hear his response.

'Well now, Rosie my love.' He leaned back in his chair giving Meggie a knowing look. She frowned and shook her head. He had his teasing face on, and she wasn't in the mood. 'You might as well ask Megs here. She met him today.' Meggie let out a frustrated sigh. Brothers!

Rose narrowed her eyes at Angus then looked at Meggie. 'Did you Meggie? What do you think of him?'

Meggie glared at Angus, then answered Rose. 'I only met him for a moment, at the door to the clinic.'

'But you must have an impression, even from a brief

meeting?' Rose may have been teasing too, Meggie wasn't sure.

Taking a sip of her wine, Meggie thought about what she could say to describe Max. A small smile played around her mouth as she looked at Rose. 'He's big.'

Rose snorted her wine, laughing. 'What? Big?' She looked at Angus for confirmation, but he gave nothing away. 'You mean, overweight big?'

'Just big. Tall. Maybe taller than Angus.' Meggie squinted at her brother, before turning back to Rose. 'But broader. Chest, shoulders. He's a giant.' Rose was laughing softly, leaning forward. Then Meggie remembered something. 'And big hands. Enormous hands.' She lifted her right hand up and waved it in front of Rose. 'Made my hand look small. Lady-like. Delicate even.'

Angus was chuckling now, and Rose threw her head back and laughed. 'Oh Meggie, what an impression he's made on you! I can't wait to meet this giant of yours.'

'He's not mine. He belongs to Angus.' Meggie lifted her glass to her lips. Darn. It was empty.

'Oh hold on girls. He's not mine. Don't make this weird now.' Angus shook his head, laughing, and lifted the wine bottle. 'Empty. Should we open another one?'

Meggie jumped in quickly. 'No. Not for me anyway. I actually want to talk to you guys about something.'

'I'll get some soda water for us Meggie. But can you wait a moment, I still want Angus to tell us about Max. About the vet stuff.' Rose walked back into the kitchen, returning with a jug of soda water and three glasses.

'He's good Rose. A good vet. He was great at the clinic

today. Has a nice way with the patients and their owners. He had Margaret O'Brien practically purring, more than that old cat of hers, and you know she's always sharp with me.' Angus crossed his legs, comfortable in the wicker chair. 'But he was great out at Drum's with the heifers today too. Not over-confident, but as soon as we had the job started he was fine. When we checked the mare, Storm, it was obvious he knows equine health, that's for sure.' Rose had leaned forward. 'And before you ask, Storm is doing well, she'll foal in about a month, we think.'

Meggie was about to speak when Angus added more quietly. 'Max told me today that his wife died in a car accident almost a year ago. That's why he has Tommy here. They're looking for a fresh start. I'd say he's a bit older than me. Late thirties perhaps.'

'Ohhh!' Meggie and Rose spoke in unison. Meggie glanced at her hand, recalling how it looked inside Max's. It's good he'd told Angus about his situation and note to self; he's unlikely to be looking for romance. And neither is she. Not yet anyway.

'Now tell us about your stuff Megs. You've been busting to all evening.' Angus patted Meggie on the shoulder.

She took a breath and started, quickly blurting it all out. About not wanting to return to the States and hoping to stay permanently in Barrington, moving into the flat to give their mum and Barry the suite at the homestead, and about the conversation with Harriet Russell and the business concept. She drew a breath and looked at them.

Angus stood up, held his arms out. Meggie rose and walked into them. He held her tightly and she felt a sob rising in her throat. 'I couldn't be happier Megs. Make this your home. See you all the time. For Mum to be able to visit both of us, and our children.' He squeezed her tight. 'No pressure. But having you nearby is the best news.'

Rose moved next to him while he spoke and somehow Meggie found herself enclosed in her arms, both sobbing. 'Just. So. Happy. When my grandfather died I had no family. Now I have a husband and Charlie, parents in-law and a sister!' Meggie's cheek touched Rose's, their tears mingling. This was what she had missed in the States. Yes, she'd made friends. But Angus, her big brother. Nothing replaced him. And Rose. A sister? Yes. All she could think was, yes.

Meggie knew there was other stuff. Stuff she wanted to leave behind in Napa Valley. It wouldn't be easy. But having a secure home and her family, that would help.

12

Tommy didn't say much on the way back to the clinic in the Vet car with Angus driving. Max knew he'd have plenty to say later. Watching Tommy say goodbye to Billie and Drum, and thank Harriet for afternoon tea, Max felt more than a little proud. Tommy had been friendly and polite, and he could see he had an affinity with Billie, racing off for another look at the horses while the adults drank their tea. But he had returned when he was called, with no fuss made.

Angus thanked Max for a good day's work when he dropped them at the back of the clinic, and Max felt he should be thanking Angus instead. But he waved as Angus backed out, then walked through to the apartment with Tommy.

'Take a shower mate, we'll walk across to the pub for a quick meal tonight.' Tommy said okay and headed to the bathroom. 'Any homework due tomorrow?'

'Nup. It was all easy stuff today. I sat with a boy called Fred Jennings. He comes to school on the bus, from further up in the mountains. He's got a lot of older brothers and they live on a big cattle farm.' Tommy paused, one hand poised to open the bathroom door. 'He was a bit of a show off and called me a city slicker at lunch time. I wanted to like him, but he was kinda rude to me in front of his brother in year six and then he teased Billie Murray.'

'Oh really? Did Billie get upset?' Max had liked the forthright little girl.

Tommy shook his head quickly. 'Not Billie. She told him she'd help with his reading if he went to the infants class to get a book he could manage. He went bright red, and she skipped away.' Tommy chuckled, then looked like he wanted to say more, so Max prompted him. 'And?'

'Nothing.' Tommy stepped into the bathroom and closed the door. Max frowned, he wondered if other kids had been cruel because he was new. He hoped Billie hadn't. Or Tiffany. That would be awkward.

Max ordered a steak and ginger beer, and Tommy had a kid-size schnitzel and a glass of lemonade. Max would have liked a real beer, it had been a busy, hot day, but he didn't want to get in the habit of having one every day. They didn't speak much while they ate but stayed after to finish their drinks.

'And was the afternoon okay at school, after Fred was rude?' Max's heart dropped as Tommy hung his head for a moment.

'I don't want to say.' This worried Max more.

'I think you should tell me Tommy, you always have

before.' He didn't want to push too hard but needed to know if there was anything brewing at school he could circumvent.

Tommy looked across at him, slightly flushed. 'Billie was right, Fred's not a very good reader. He's almost a year older than me and doing the year three work, while I'm already on year four stuff.' He stopped, looking distressed for a moment. 'Fred tried to look at my maths, and I covered it with my elbow. He kicked my foot under the desk.'

Max considered his answer for a moment. 'Well Tommy, letting Fred copy your work wouldn't really help him learn, so you did the right thing. But you also know that you find a lot of schoolwork easier than others do, so you shouldn't tease him about it.'

'I didn't tease him. But Miss Bolitho saw him kick me and she moved me to another desk and now I'm sitting in a three, not a two.' Tommy had tears in his eyes.

'What's a three?'

'The desks are in twos and some threes. I'm at a three at the back now. It's for the kids doing the year four work.' He still seemed upset.

'Is that a problem? You already said it wasn't too hard for you.' Max was confused but needed to get to the source of Tommy's unease.

Tommy hung his head again and muttered something.

'Tell me, Tommy. What's bothering you? Don't you like who you're sitting with now?'

Tommy looked up, his eyes bright with unshed tears. 'That's just it Dad, I do like who I'm sitting with. Billie and Tiffany.' He wiped his eyes with his arm. 'But they're girls! I've never been friends with girls before!'

Relief washed over Max, but he tried not to let it show on his face. 'Well Tommy, I don't think it matters much. From what I saw of Billie this afternoon, she was happy to feed the horses and show you around the farm. It's not like she asked you to go to a doll's tea party, is it?'

'No. She's great. She knows about lots of farm stuff, especially horses and she even said she'd let me ride one of hers next time.' He shook his head slowly. 'I'd really like that, but I don't want to get teased about playing with girls, you know, at school.'

'Tiffany's mum already told me that the boys and girls at Barrington don't seem to care, and often play together. I don't think it's a problem Tommy, and you're sure to make friends with some boys too, although maybe not Fred.' He watched as Tommy digested this, then looked up, happier now.

'So it's alright then? That I'm friends with Billie and Tiffany?'

'It's better than alright. It's perfect. Billie's Dad is one of our best clients and Tiffany's mum is our Vet Nurse.' He reached across, ruffling his hair. 'Come on mate, we've got time to watch a bit of the tennis before you go to bed.' Tommy grinned then and finished his lemonade in one big gulp.

They strolled back to their flat, and Tommy was asleep before the tennis really got started. Max turned the television off and sat on the couch for a while, casually looking at real estate in the area on his iPad. He had a good feeling about it, but it was a bit soon to make anything permanent.

13

Meggie made some healthy snacks first thing in the morning, supervising Charlie while she worked. Debbie, Melanie and Harriet were coming at three for their first look at Rose's wedding dress, and Rose had laughed when Meggie asked about afternoon tea and said she wouldn't eat anything at all between now and the wedding if she wanted the dress to fit. It had arrived at the courier depot the night before and Rose rushed into town after breakfast to pick it up. Meggie hadn't seen it and was really curious, and when she asked Debbie if she knew the style she'd shaken her head. 'No, Rose hasn't given me any hints at all, although with her height and figure she can wear any style she chooses.'

In fact, Rose hadn't been keen to show anyone the dress, wanting to keep it a total surprise. But Meggie had gently advised they needed to see it to make sure they found a bridesmaid dress for Debbie that worked with it, and to ensure the simple decorations for the wedding fitted with her chosen style. She'd given in, then become quite excited and wanted Harriet and Melanie to see it too. Debbie's mother-in-law Jill was coming to pick up Charlie at lunch-time, keeping him for the afternoon.

The day flew by, Rose rushed home, carrying the large, well-wrapped clothing bag to her room. They had a light lunch after Charlie was picked up and spent some time running through Meggie's initial ideas, and budget, for the wedding. Meggie suggested an elegant white and rose gold theme, with pops of colour provided by roses from the garden, set around the marquee. Low vases on the tables and a few tall vases on plinths near the entrance and each side of the dance floor. She wouldn't introduce another colour until she saw the wedding dress, although she assumed it would be white. Rose still needed to choose a style and colour for Debbie.

'I love it Meggie, thank you.' Rose clapped her hands, 'you're brilliant at this. I wouldn't have known where to start but this is perfect. I hope you love the wedding dress, 'cos I think it fits with the theme too.'

Nodding happily, Meggie felt a small glow of pleasure. She wanted the day to be perfect for Angus and Rose and was thrilled to be involved.

Debbie, Harriet and Melanie arrived after three, with two bottles of French champagne. Debbie held one aloft as she rushed in. 'Girl time! I don't care that it's only for a couple of hours, I'm so excited to see your dress Rose.' She set the bottle down, reached up and hugged Rose tightly. Harriet and Melanie laughed as they entered.

'Jill has Charlie and Woz, does she have Tiffany too?' Meggie looked at the women as Rose asked the question.

'No, Tiffany and Tommy went home on the bus with Billie. Drum's giving them all a riding lesson. Melanie will pick up Tiff and Tommy when we're done here.' Harriet said this with a chuckle. 'I left some afternoon tea for them all, but I think Drum will have his hands full. Tommy's a beginner and Billie will want to help with his lesson.' The five women looked at each other and laughed.

'Now Rose, you need to get this dress on, we can't wait to see what you've chosen.' This was from Debbie, who then leaned toward Meggie, saying in a loud whisper, 'she didn't invite her best friend to go wedding shopping, so you know, she might just have white pants and a tee.' Meggie giggled, then quickly looked at Rose in case she was offended. But she was laughing with all of them.

'Oh come on. I dress up. Sometimes. When the occasion calls for it.' Rose shook her head, wagging a finger at Debbie. 'You don't think I've got any style at all. But wait, you'll see.'

Debbie wagged a finger back at Rose. 'Rose darling. You are a stunning woman and would look good in a hessian bag. But I don't want you wearing one down the aisle.' They all giggled, and Meggie relaxed. These women genuinely care for each other, and she felt sure Rose had chosen something special, her excitement was palpable.

Head high, Rose pointed to the champagne glasses on the kitchen bench, along with the small platter of snacks Meggie had made earlier. 'Pour the bubbles girls, while I transform into a bride.' She turned toward the hallway.

Meggie called out, 'do you need a hand Rose, to get into it?'

Rose stopped, turned back to them. 'Probably. I will on the day. But today I want to surprise you all. Talk amongst yourselves please, I will return.'

Meggie poured the drinks and ensured the others had something to eat. The women included her in their conversation, and she relaxed. Her ears pricked up when Melanie mentioned Max.

'He's a good Vet, the clients and patients have taken to him. He said the clients are not always as easy to get on with in the city practice, always stressed and busy. Says he loves it here already. Tommy is a really nice kid and sits with Billie and Tiffany in class.'

'Is he divorced or separated? Is that why they're on they're own?' Harriet asked quietly.

Melanie shook her head. 'His wife died in a car accident. He told Angus on the first day, but you know Angus, he didn't say a thing to me. Then Tiffany told me. Tommy told the girls when they asked where his Mum is.' She paused, 'apparently Billie told him her mum lives in England, and she never sees her either.' Melanie glanced at Harriet. 'Then she said she has Harriet now and she's a lot more fun.'

Harriet snort-laughed with a mouthful of champagne, then wiped a tear from her eye. 'Love that kid. Billie.'

Movement caught their attention. Rose walked toward them, and they gave a collective, 'ohh!' She wore a rose gold silk satin gown, with an off-the-shoulder low cut sweetheart neckline, fitted to the waist, then draped softly from her waist to the floor. She turned in a circle, the back dipped in a low cowl to almost her bottom cleavage, held together by a delicate criss-cross of matching chain.

Meggie felt tears spring to her eyes. Rose looked beautiful, the dress absolutely perfect for her. It clung to her in all the right places and had an old-Hollywood-glam look about it. Meggie squinted thoughtfully as the other women moved toward Rose, touching the fabric, exclaiming and clapping their hands, turning her around for another look at the back.

Rose looked over their heads, meeting Meggie's gaze. She looked unsure. 'What do *you* think Megs?' They all turned to Meggie. She stood, walked toward Rose, almost in tears. Rose had never called her Megs before, always Meggie. A wave of affection for her soon-to-be-sister-in-law washed over her and she touched Rose's face. 'Spectacular. Original. Stunning.' She was rewarded by a happy smile from Rose. 'This dress. It's perfect for you. It's totally old Hollywood glam. Seriously, movie star Rita Hayworth could have worn this to the Oscars. Wherever did you find it? The material, the style. It's nothing short of superb.'

Rose grinned at Debbie. 'The vintage bridal store in Sydney where we found Debbie's dress. I loved what Debbie wore to her wedding.' She turned to Meggie. 'It was a nineteen fifties tea-length gown. But when I tried them on they didn't suit. I'm too tall, the skirts too full. So the stylist took me into the nineteen forties room, where everything was satin and slinky. I tried on about ten, but this one, the colour I think, stood out for me.' She giggled. 'And the back is a little bit sexy. I feel like a siren or a sex goddess, in this dress.' She thrust her chest out a bit. 'It's even got a built-in pointy brassiere.' She looked again at Meggie. 'I was thinking

Katherine Hepburn may have worn something like this, but Rita Hayworth is better, she had auburn hair too!' She laughed, pointing to her own thick hair, which she had pulled into a loose bun at her neck.

Meggie looked at Debbie, thick blonde hair and a few inches shorter than Rose. 'Stand next to Rose for a moment please Deb.' Debbie moved to Rose's side, they giggled at each other. Meggie moved between Harriet and Melanie, linking her arms through theirs, facing Rose and Debbie. 'I'm thinking navy blue for Deb, similar sweetheart neckline in front but not the low back, then pinched in at the waist like Rose's dress, but ending in a neat pencil skirt mid-calf. Nineteen forties peep-toe-pumps in navy. What do you think?'

'Yes!' They all spoke at once and Rose spun around happily. 'I can see that. I can really see that. I love it Meggie.' She turned around. 'I'd better get out of this dress now. I'm dying for a glass of champagne.'

'Wait.' Meggie was scrolling through her phone. 'Do you have any fixed ideas about what Angus should wear? And Jamie, as his best man?'

Rose nodded. 'Black tie, I thought.'

'Perfect. Black tie it is. We've moved from simple elegance to something a little more glam, but I can work with that.' Meggie and the others agreed, all chatting at once.

Rose took a step back, and spun in a full circle, until she was facing them again. She was radiant. 'I'm getting married girls, I'm really getting married!' They cheered. 'Megs, can you come and help me get out of this please, I'm terrified I'll step on the hem and tear it.'

Meggie followed Rose to her room. She gently undid the

zip hidden in the side of the dress, then lifted it over her head. Rose turned to get dressed while Meggie carefully returned the gown to the clothing bag. Meggie lay the clothing bag across the bed and was about to leave, but Rose was dressed now. She stepped forward and hugged Meggie, saying quietly in her ear. 'I've always wanted a sister.'

Tears sprang to Meggie's eyes, her face beside Rose's. 'Me too, Rose, me too.' They stepped back, gazing happily at each other. Then Rose picked up the dress in its protective bag and thrust it at Meggie. 'Hang it in your room, I don't want Angus to have the slightest idea.' Meggie touched her hand gently and took the dress.

14

Two weeks in and Max had settled into a routine, with work and Tommy. He was handling most of the clinic work now, with Angus spending more time on his own farm. They were doing the large animal work together, but not every afternoon, so Max sat with Melanie some days to learn the patient filing system and accounts. He'd picked Tommy and Tiffany up from school several times, giving Melanie a chance to do her shopping and run errands. It was working well, and the kids were great. He wasn't comfortable taking Tiffany to the flat, it was so small, so he generally let them help him in the animal hospital and took them to Debbie's café for afternoon tea.

The highlight of Tommy's week was going home on the bus with Billie and Tiffany, where Drum Murray gave him a riding lesson. Max had driven out after work with Melanie to pick them up and had been impressed at how confident Tommy was on the part-Arab pony called Chippy. Billie was on a larger horse called Lady, and Max knew in an instant she'd been riding for years. Tiffany said she usually rode Chippy, but she seemed happy to let Tommy have a turn.

'I've been at Rose and Angus's this afternoon, you know, wedding dress stuff.' Melanie chatted as they drove out to the Murray farm. Max nodded. That's why he'd been hired. The wedding was only a few weeks away, then Angus and Rose would be away for their honeymoon. 'Rose would like you and Tommy to go out to their place for dinner on Saturday night. It'll be us, you met my husband Ben the other day, Drum, Harriet and Billie, and Debbie from the café with her husband Jamie and their baby boy. And Rose and Angus of course, and I think you met Meggie, Angus's sister the other day too.' He was about to decline, it sounded like a group of long-time friends to him. But Melanie continued, 'Angus will also ask you, but Rose wanted you to know the invitation is really from her. She's keen for you and Tommy to be there.'

'Alright.' He smiled at Melanie, they were pulling up at Drum's horse yards. 'It would be rude to say no, wouldn't it?'

'You betcha.' Melanie stepped out, put her arm around Tiffany who had walked across to the car. Max strolled to the fence with them. Drum was standing in the centre of the round yard, supervising Tommy on a grey pony. Tommy was wearing a hard hat and the biggest grin. He had the reins firmly in his hands and Max knew he would have waved if he could. Billie, on tip toes, was unsaddling her horse by the fence. Tiffany followed Billie into the stables, carrying the saddle blanket for her.

'Ride over to the fence Tommy, say hi to your dad.' Drum called out from the centre of yards. Tommy turned the horse, touched his heels to its side, and trotted over to where Max stood, rising correctly in the saddle as he did. Drum strolled across too, putting one foot on the bottom rail, he patted the horse on the shoulder. 'He's a natural Max. Took to it straight away. Cowboy potential.'

Max chuckled, looking from Tommy's happy face to Drum. 'Thank you Drum. Really. Very good of you.'

'It's what we do. He's a good kid.' He turned to Tommy. 'Ride over to the gate, Billie will help you unsaddle Chippy. Then I'd like you to brush him down and give him some feed.'

'Yes Mr Murray.' Tommy turned the horse and trotted to the gate, where Billie and Tiffany had reappeared.

'Angus tells me you've lightened the load considerably. He said he's barely been into the clinic this week.' Drum chuckled as he spoke, and Max warmed to him.

'It's a good business, it's easy to work somewhere that's clean and organised.' He glanced at Melanie beside him, 'although I suspect the organised part is all Melanie.'

She laughed. 'You do all right Max Masters.'

* * *

FRIDAY AFTERNOON MELANIE PICKED TOMMY UP WITH TIFFANY, she was taking them to the library after school, then home for afternoon tea. Tommy was keen to see where Tiffany lived, they had a small farm too and some new kittens.

Max stepped out of the clinic, locking the door. Melanie wouldn't drop Tommy back for another hour, so he thought he'd pick up something from the shops for dinner. He'd bought an air fryer for the flat, so chops and chips in it, with carrots and peas done in the microwave. The fridge was tiny, so he only bought what they needed every couple of days.

With time up his sleeve, Max crossed the road, the supermarket was next to the Post Office, with a lane between them. Movement in the lane caught his eye. Meggie Hamilton was dragging a large suitcase out of the back of an old Landrover, and as he watched she tripped and fell, with the suitcase squarely on top of her.

He rushed to help her, lifting the suitcase off, holding his hand out to pull her up. He noticed how pretty she was when she blushed. 'Thanks Max. Just as well you saw me, I might have been stuck under there for days, weeks even.' She laughed, brushing herself off ruefully. Max caught his breath. She was gorgeous. Tall, thick dark hair and right now, dancing brown eyes.

He laughed with her. 'All part of the service, Ms Hamilton, Ma'am.' Doffing an imaginary hat. He looked around. 'Where are you taking this beast?' He saw another suitcase in the back of the car, and a couple of boxes.

'Upstairs. To the flat over the post office. My mum and step-father arrive on Sunday, and I've rented the flat, you know, to make more room at the homestead.' She pointed toward the staircase behind the lovely old sandstone building. 'There are back stairs, thought it might be easier than taking everything through the front entrance.'

'I'll carry these up for you.' He could see she was about to decline, obviously an independent woman, but she looked up at the stairs, then at the two suitcases.

'Okay, that's brilliant, thanks.' She picked up one of the

boxes from the back seat and he followed her up the stairs with the first suitcase. She unlocked the door and stepped in, holding it open so he could bring the suitcase through. His shoulder touched hers as he entered, and he could smell her perfume, which confused him for a moment.

'Um, Max?' He turned when she spoke. She pointed to the suitcase, her smile broad. 'it's got wheels, I can take it from here.'

'Of course.' He set it down, then almost ran back down the stairs, hauling the second case out of the vehicle. She followed him down, picked up the other box, and walked up the stairs in front of him again. He took his time, watching her shapely bottom, encased in denim cut-offs, as she took each stair. Long legs, nice bum, small waist. She had turned before he reached the top. Her look was questioning. She'd caught him looking at her backside. Damn. She'd know by now that he was widowed.

He placed the case on its wheels as he walked through the door, pushing it a few feet into the room.

'Thanks Max, appreciate that.' She looked at him, and he wondered if she was going to ask about his wife. 'Where's Tommy this afternoon?'

He let out a small breath. 'Melanie picked him up with Tiffany. He's gone to see some new kittens. Much more exciting than hanging with me.'

Laughing, she turned, pushing the second case further into what looked like a laundry room. 'Kittens. They'll do it every time.'

He stood awkwardly for a moment, knowing he should leave her to unpack. He was curious about the apartment.

And about her, he admitted to himself. 'Any chance I could take the tour? I love these old buildings.'

'Um. Sure. Come in.' He followed her in, and she closed the back door, leading him through a large room to the front door.

'Let's start here. You come through the door to this fabulous big room. Kitchen down on the far wall. Lots of natural light.' He was fascinated, she lit up when she spoke about the history of the building, the changes that had been made to the apartment over the years. He followed her through to the bedrooms, they were enormous, and the bathroom was relatively modern.

Back in the centre of the living area he walked to the windows overlooking the main street. 'Right across the road from the clinic.' His smile was wide. 'If I'd seen it first I might have snapped it up.'

'Yes, Angus said the flat at the clinic is very small, not much more than a motel room really. How are you and Tommy coping?' She seemed genuinely interested, so he told her.

'It's great. It works for now, with Angus soon to be away, we need someone there if we have overnight patients. The kitchen isn't much, but I bought an air fryer, so we don't eat out every night.' He chuckled, 'I'm not a great cook, but I can manage a couple of chops and chips. And it's fine for breakfast and lunch.'

'But you said you would have taken this if you'd known. Are you looking to stay, after Angus gets back?' she prompted him.

'Well. Yes, I'd like to. I like the area and Tommy is

enjoying school. We're meeting people. But Angus hasn't asked me to stay, and I don't want him to feel pressured.' He suddenly felt concerned. This is a conversation he should have with Angus, not his sister.

She nudged him with her shoulder, speaking quietly. 'I get it Max. He won't hear it from me. But honestly?' He nodded and she continued. 'I think Angus is hoping you'll want to stay, so keep doing what you do, it may work out exactly the way you want it to.'

He felt suddenly lighter. While it hadn't come from Angus himself, he didn't think Meggie would say it without reason. 'Are you staying here tonight Meggie, or will you wait until Sunday when your family arrives?'

He saw the happy look on her face. 'Oh, I'm staying here. I have bedding in those boxes and some kitchen things borrowed from Rose. The fridge is on, and I have a bottle of wine cooling. I'm going to make the bed, unpack some gear, then whip up something simple for dinner,' she leaned closer, 'like a vegemite sandwich, and toast my new home.'

'Sounds brilliant Meggie.' He took another look out the window, such a great position. 'And you, Meggie. Are you settling into the area or is this just short-term accommodation until the wedding?' Her face lit up when he asked, she intrigued him in a way he hadn't felt about a woman in a long time.

'I'm staying. I'm setting up a business here. Weddings and events, and maybe festivals and such.' She pointed across the road to Evans Real Estate, a few doors up from the Vet Clinic. 'Harriet has offered me office space, and we're planning to collaborate on some things.' She glanced at Max. 'Maybe it's a fresh start, here in Barrington, for both of us.'

Her words made him happy, he didn't want to think about the reason for that, not yet anyway. He glanced at his watch. 'Thanks for the tour, Melanie will be dropping Tommy back shortly, so I'd better head across the road.'

'Thank you. For the grunt work.' She cocked her head to one side, cheekily. Something about the way she said grunt sent a rush of blood to his groin. He turned toward the door, he needed to leave. Now. But as he reached the door, he turned back to her. She was right there, in front of him.

'I'm taking Tommy to the pub for a quick dinner, you know, Friday night special. You're welcome to join us.' He really hoped she'd say yes. 'Not as good as a vegemite sandwich, to be sure, but we could share a bottle of wine and celebrate your new home.' His earlier thoughts of chops in the air fryer deserted him.

He watched as she considered his question. 'Sure. Why not. I've heard some good things about Tommy, I'd love to meet him.' He knew she was teasing him, knew too that she felt something, a connection between them.

'Six o'clock then. Want us to pick you up?'

'Ha, ha, the pub is four doors that way. Thank you, but I'll meet you there at six.' She stepped back, then added, 'don't you lads stand me up now.'

He threw back his head and laughed. 'Not a chance, Meggie, not a chance.'

15

Meggie leant against the door, hearing him clatter down the stairs two at a time. What was she thinking? He's widowed, with a young son. She should cool her jets. But she'd flirted, a little. Maybe to see if she could, you know, get a reaction from him. Had he flirted back? She thought so, but maybe he was being nice because he wants it to work out at the clinic with Angus.

She walked to the window, watched him cross the street. He didn't go through the front of the clinic but walked down the side lane to the back. She hadn't met Tommy, but Melanie said he was lovely, and friends with her daughter Tiffany and Harriet's ... um, what is Billie to Harri? Step-daughter? Not quite, they're not married. But she could hear Harri's love for Billie when she spoke of her. Step-daughter works.

Max was a few years older than her, closer to forty than thirty. She'd been with an older man before, back in Napa. It hadn't worked out. She had wasted two years, ruined her career and alienated some very good work friends. And she'd lost something she may never have again. A small sob escaped her. She stepped back. Yes, she'd have dinner with him and Tommy. Get to know them, they'd be part of the fabric of her community if they stayed, but she shouldn't get involved. Wouldn't get involved.

Walking quickly to the main bedroom, she made up the bed, then unpacked one of the suitcases. She'd have a quick shower and change. She hung some dresses in the wardrobe, and noticed how most of them were short, to show her legs to best advantage, or fitted to show off her figure. She thought for a moment about Rose's wedding dress. A similar height and shape to herself, the style was something that Meggie had once dreamed of. She'd organised so many weddings, seen so many brides, but Rose in that dress, not just glamorous, but simply elegant.

It was almost six and she was still trying to decide what to wear. In the end she took a shapeless shift from its hanger. It was plain cream, sleeveless and almost reached her knees, with a row of sunflowers around the hem. Flat sandals, a touch of mascara and lip-gloss, hair in a high messy bun and she was ready. She picked up her small crossover bag and walked down the main stairs to the street.

It was five past six when she stepped into the air-conditioned dining room at the pub. Max waved to her from a booth to one side. She waved back and walked over. He stood. Then she saw Tommy. A miniature version of his father, his hair freshly washed and brushed to one side. He stood and waited beside his dad. She was delighted.

'Hi Meggie, this is Tommy.'

Tommy held his hand out, saying, 'Hello Meggie,' as he did. She took his hand, he shook hers with a firm little grip.

'Hello Tommy, nice to meet you too. Hi Max.'

Tommy sat down and slid over, Max moved in beside him, offering Meggie the seat on the other side of the table, then handed her the wine list. 'You will know the wines better than I.' His fingers brushed hers as she took it, making her catch her breath for a moment. She wondered if he felt something too, but he didn't let on.

'It's a warm night, and I don't get too concerned about matching my wine to my meal, so I think a Sauvignon Blanc works best.' She looked up at him. 'If that suits you?'

'Excellent. I'll go to the bar while you have a look at the menu.' He leaned toward his son. 'Tommy can't decide between the lamb chops and the chicken schnitzel.'

As Max walked to the bar she glanced at the menu, then turned to Tommy. 'Have you tried both meals before?'

He nodded vigorously. 'Yup. We've eaten here eight times in two weeks, and I've tried almost everything. But they have a specials board,' he pointed to a blackboard leaning against the wall, 'and they have duck spring rolls as an entrée. I think I'll order that tonight, you know, as my main course.'

Great kid. Articulate too. She raised an eyebrow at him. 'Do you want to get the duck spring rolls as an entrée, and share them with me, then we can get a main course each too?'

His expression became serious, as he considered this. Max was returning to the table with the drinks. 'Yes please!' He reached for the glass of orange juice Max passed across, then looked over at Meggie. 'Thank you.'

Max poured the wine, offering a glass to Meggie. She

lifted it to her nose, breathing in the crisp citrus tones. Max raised his glass, clinked with Tommy and then Meggie. 'What is my son thanking you for, Meggie Hamilton?' She chuckled at his use of her full name, his voice was deep, rich with emotion. She could clearly see his devotion for Tommy. It made him more attractive to her, but she shook her head slightly, telling herself to get that thought out of her mind.

'No? You don't want to tell me?' Now his words were full of laughter. Tommy nudged his father. 'I'm ordering the duck spring rolls.' Max was about to speak, but Tommy continued. 'Meggie said she'd share the entrée with me, then I'll have the kids chicken schnitty.'

'Oh, did she?' he picked up the menu Tommy handed him. 'And what would you like for main course Meggie?' He looked over the menu, meeting her eyes.

'The Caesar Salad, with chicken. But I'll get it, you've already bought the drinks.'

Max looked at his son for a moment. Tommy cleared his throat, then spoke quite seriously to Meggie. 'Masters men don't let girls pay for their own dinner.' She almost laughed.

'Really? Well in that case, thank you very much, er Masters men.' Tommy pulled his glass closer, taking a big sip. Max slid out of the booth. 'I'll order.' She could see he was proud of his boy, was raising him to have manners. She liked that. She watched him stride back to the bar. He wore blue jeans and loafers and an open neck shirt. He looked good in those jeans from behind, and she had been trying not to stare at the size of his shoulders, and arms since she sat down. He was a giant, even taller than Angus and a fraction broader.

Focus on Tommy, she told herself. 'How was school today Tommy?'

'Good thank you.' He sipped his drink. She tried again. 'What was the best part of your day?' Tommy thought for a moment, then his face split into a broad grin. 'Playing with Tiffany's kittens. I'm going to be a Vet too when I grow up. I'll be Dad's partner.'

'Will you? That's an excellent plan.' She watched Max return. 'And do you need to do a lot of study to be a Vet?'

'Years and years. School, then uni. I'm good at maths and science, and Vet's need that.' His little face was animated. She was entranced. Max was turned slightly toward his son. He's heard this before, she was sure, but he was taking a keen interest in the boy's words. 'And I'm going to specialise in equine health.' He leaned toward Meggie. 'That's horses.'

'It's great you know what you want to do Tommy. That will keep you motivated along the way.'

Max topped Meggie's glass up. 'And you Meggie. Did you always want to go into event management?'

'I studied hotel management and communications at Uni. I really wanted to travel. And I'm very organised. I worked in hotels in Melbourne and Sydney, then London for a while. Then four years in California in the Napa Valley.'

He actively listened as she spoke. She had his full attention. 'And now, here in Barrington. It will be quieter for you, but I totally understand wanting to start your own business, be the master of your destiny. You'll make it work, I'm sure.' She was warmed by his praise, and wanted to continue the conversation, but realised it left Tommy out.

'Tell me more about the horses you like Tommy? Have

you ridden very much?' He told her, in great detail, about his visit to Billie's farm and his ride on Chippy. But not just the ride, the grooming, saddling, and feeding the horses too. She loved the expressions on his face as he described his experience, and at one point Max hastily moved the half-full glass of orange juice away from his hands, as he was demonstrating how he had lifted the saddle off his horse. She found herself laughing, asking for more details. Max said very little, and she had almost forgotten his presence, until he nudged Tommy, saying, 'your entrée is here.'

While they ate Max spoke a little bit about his first two weeks in the area and told some entertaining anecdotes about some of his patients, including a very angry blue-tongue lizard. The entree came with three spring rolls, so Tommy offered a second one to Meggie. She declined, saying she wouldn't eat her main course. He then offered it to his dad. Max ruffled his hair. 'You eat it son, I've got a steak coming.'

By seven thirty they'd finished the wine, and dinner, and Tommy was starting to yawn, but covered his mouth, saying excuse me, each time.

Meggie covered her own mouth, as if yawning. 'It's been lovely, Masters men, but I need to get my beauty sleep.' They all slid out of the booth, Max and Tommy waiting for her to walk ahead of them. They strolled with her to the downstairs entrance to her flat, waiting while she unlocked the door.

'Goodnight, thank you for dinner.'

'Goodnight Meggie.' Tommy and Max spoke at the same time, then looked at each other and laughed.

'I think we're catching up again tomorrow, at Angus and Rose's house, so I'll see you there.' Meggie stepped inside.

'Bye, see you tomorrow!' This was from Tommy.

She ran quickly up the stairs, opened her front door, then dashed to the window, pulling the heavy drapes to one side. Max had his arm around Tommy's shoulders, they were almost to the other side of the street, Tommy was speaking to his father, his young face looking earnestly up at him. They reached the entrance to the side lane and Max stopped, looked up to her window. She was about to step back, but he raised his hand in a wave. She waved back, then quickly pulled the curtains closed.

16

Tommy was in bed five minutes after they got home, so Max relaxed on the sofa in semi-darkness with a cold beer and thought about the last two weeks, how quickly they had settled in at Barrington. But his mind drifted, from Barrington, to the Vet practice, to Angus, hoping Meggie was right and there was a real possibility they could stay. Maybe he could buy into the practice if Angus was interested. He'd already sold his share of the Newcastle clinic, three of his former partners had been great, made it easy for him. Not the fourth partner though. He shook his head. Don't go down that path, not tonight.

His mind rattled around for a few minutes, putting away bad memories. He chuckled, it was a game he played with himself, picturing his mind opening a new file to store new memories, good memories, locking the old ones in the bottom drawer of a virtual filing cabinet. He was almost ready to toss away the key to that drawer. It was something the therapist had suggested to Tommy, but Max thought he'd benefited more.

So now he had a bright shiny new drawer, with Meggie's name on the front. Images of her chatting with Tommy, laughing at something he said. Her long legs in cut off shorts, walking up the stairs ahead of him; laughing as he lifted the suitcase and helped her off the ground; waving from the upstairs window when he looked back. He finished his beer, placing the empty bottle in the bin. He looked at Tommy, asleep in the bed. When it first happened, the kid wouldn't sleep until Max lay down with him, would curl up against him, needing to know his dad was right there. But now, here, he was sprawled in the bed, one foot sticking out beneath the covers, sleeping soundly. As he should, Max thought, as he should.

He picked up his phone, checked for messages. Nothing. He sent one anyway.

We're loving it here, would be great to have you visit. His finger hovered over the buttons. *Love you.* XX

No reply. He didn't really expect one, but he remained hopeful.

MAX WONDERED IF HE SHOULD TAKE SOMETHING TO THE barbecue. He'd asked Angus the day before, and he'd said, 'Nah, mate, it's just a steak on the barbie, sausages for the kids. The girls will have salads organised.' He wondered if he should take a bottle of wine, and definitely some beer, although he wouldn't drink much himself, he needed to drive home.

He strolled down to the café with Tommy. They'd been up early and taken a football to the park, where they'd spent a happy couple of hours kicking it around before it got too hot. When Tommy said he wanted to stop, needing a cold drink, Max happily obliged.

The café was busy, so they found a seat outside. Tommy waited there while Max walked in to order.

'Hey Max, how are you?' Debbie waved at him from the coffee machine.

'Great, thanks. You're busy today. Or is this the usual summer weekend?' He gestured to the interior of the café, humming with chatter.

'It's busier than usual, but with all the rain recently the rivers are up and there's a lot of people in town for the outdoor stuff. You know, kayaking, bushwalking to the falls.' She passed two coffees to a younger member of staff, then stepped over to the cash register. 'What would the Masters men like today?'

Max chuckled. Tommy had started it, but it was catching on. 'Tommy wants his favourite milkshake, and a big brownie.' He leaned forward. 'He emphasised big. And I'll have an Americano and apple slice please.'

'We can do that. I've got an oversize brownie out in the kitchen, two of them stuck together when Cathy baked earlier. I'll send it out.' Debbie beamed, taking his payment.

'Careful, you might set a precedent and he'll want double size every time.' Max strolled back to the table, a couple of clients said hello as he did. That hardly ever happened in Newcastle. As he sat, the phone in his pocket vibrated. It was a text. Tommy leaned closer to see it, but Max gave him a look and he sat back.

Hey Max, it's Rose. Don't bring anything tonight. But come early, around 4pm, and Tommy can visit my horses.

Nice. He liked Rose, had only met her a couple of times, but she was friendly and direct. He shook his head at Tommy. 'It's Rose. Wants us to come early to visit her horses. What do you think?'

'Answer her Dad! Tell her yes please!' Tommy fist-pumped the air.

Thanks Rose. You've made Tommy's day! See you at 4. Max.

But he wouldn't go empty-handed. He looked at Tommy. 'When we finish here, let's buy the biggest box of chocolates we can, to take there today. As a thank you.'

'Okay.' Tommy turned his attention back to the double brownie. He had chocolate on his hands and around his mouth, but he was happy, so Max quietly sipped his coffee and watched his boy enjoy himself.

17

Putting the freshly made pasta salad in the fridge, Meggie turned and stretched. It was almost four and she needed to quickly change for the barbecue. Most were arriving at five, but Max was coming early with Tommy, to see the horses. Thinking about Max made her draw a quick breath, but she remonstrated with herself. *He's grieving the loss of his wife and has responsibilities while I, well, I am not ready to risk my heart again.*

She dashed to the guest room to change into the pale blue gingham shift dress she'd brought, falling almost to the knee. It was sleeveless, showing her toned, tanned shoulders to advantage. She teamed it with flat sandals, brushed her hair and applied lip gloss and mascara. Stepping back, she looked at herself in the mirror. Feminine yet casual, she didn't want to overdo it, she was sure Rose, and the others would be similarly dressed. At the last minute she lifted her hair into a messy bun on top of her head.

Voices at the front door alerted her to Max and Tommy's arrival. She walked down the hallway, joining Angus, and Rose with Charlie on her hip. Max watched her approach, his look seemed intense for a moment, then he smiled, his eyes crinkling at the corners. Rose was holding a giant box of Belgian chocolates and Angus a bottle of wine, gifts from their guests, she thought.

Tommy grinned at her, excitement evident on his face. 'Hello Meggie. The Masters men have arrived!'

Gorgeous kid. She laughed. 'I can see that Tommy Masters.' Turning to Max, she added, 'And Max.'

'Nice to see you Meggie.' Then he focussed on Angus and Rose, 'what a beautiful home you have. Late 1800's?'

Meggie watched Rose nod happily. 'It is. My great-grand-father built it. I'll give you the tour if you like.'

Max was keen, but looked down at Tommy, who had tugged on his hand. 'Perhaps we can tour the horses first, Tommy's been bursting with excitement all day.'

Rose threw her head back and laughed. 'Of course.' She looked at Tommy. 'You have your priorities right, Tommy. Horses always come first.'

Turning to Meggie, Rose moved Charlie from one hip to the other. 'Do you think you could watch Charlie while we go to the stables Megs?' Meggie had planned to walk down with them, but she immediately held out her arms for Charlie, who threw himself into them, saying 'Megs. Megs play now.'

Angus nudged her as he walked by, setting the chocolates and wine on the hall stand. Meggie suspected he had seen the look Max had given her. He would tease her later but was unlikely to say anything to embarrass his guest. She jiggled

Charlie in her arms, making him giggle, then walked through to the living area where he had his blocks and farm animals. By the time she set him down on the floor, the front door had closed.

Keeping an eye on Charlie, now absorbed in a game involving horses, cows and a seemingly rogue giraffe, Meggie took the chocolates and wine to the kitchen. It was an excellent bottle of Australian red, from Tyrrells Wines in the Hunter region. She really should do a trip across there after the wedding, it was only a couple of hours away.

Back with Charlie, she lay on the floor on her tummy, loading animals in his toy truck, before driving them across his legs to the other side of the mat. He chortled each time, shouting, 'Again Megs, do it again!' She was laughing with him, enjoying the game, and didn't hear the others return. Charlie yelled, 'Daddee,' and ran as fast as his chubby legs would allow, across the room to Angus, standing shoulder to shoulder with Max, who was studying her intently. Flushed, Meggie got up from the floor as elegantly, and modestly, as she could, but her hair had come out of its bun during the game, and she knew she looked a red hot mess.

Mumbling something about, 'just fix my hair,' she dashed past, now seeing more people arriving through the open front door.

18

Max turned to say hello to Ben, Melanie, Drum, Harriet, Tiffany and Billie who had arrived together in Drum's large Range Rover.

'Can we play outside please Rose?' This was Billie, dressed in shorts, tee and canvas shoes, her hair in a braid down her back. Tiffany was almost identically dressed and when Rose said yes, of course, they shot across the room and out through cedar and glass doors to the back veranda. Tommy looked bemused and remained by Max's side, but within seconds Billie re-opened the door. 'Come on Tommy, you have to see the garden out here, we're going to play cricket.' Tommy looked at Max for permission. He ruffled his son's hair and said, 'Masters men never keep the ladies waiting.' Tommy walked quickly to the door, where Billie grabbed his hand and almost dragged him outside, closing the door after him.

The adults looked at each other and laughed. Melanie

nudged Max, 'he fits in well with those two. Billie is a bit of a tomboy and Tiffany loves to play sport.' Max agreed. He had wondered if he'd feel a bit uncomfortable, all these people had known each other a long time, some of them their whole lives, but the conversation was easy. Debbie and husband Jamie arrived then, their young son Warwick only just walking. He watched as Meggie and Debbie set Warwick up with Charlie on the mat with toy farm animals, then he accepted a beer from Angus and joined the men by the barbecue on the veranda. He could see the kids had set up a cricket pitch on the green lawn, and with the sun starting to go down the day had cooled.

The women joined them on the veranda, where a large table had been set at one end, with comfortable wicker chairs. Debbie and Rose moved Charlie and Warwick out to the lawn with some of their toys. Max turned around, he wanted to talk with Meggie some more, but she had disappeared inside. He turned back, to find himself face to face with Angus. He gave him a look, not unfriendly, but cautious. Max nodded to Angus, acknowledging the look, then answered a question from Jamie. Internally he noted he should be careful with Meggie. Angus was protective of his sister. But she returned from inside with two plates of cheese and crackers, setting one down on the table with the women and offered the other to the men, as she stood with them for a moment. He watched as she chatted easily among them. Smart and confident, she joined a conversation about economic development in the region, the conversation becoming animated. She fascinated him.

Harriet called out from the table, 'come on blokes. Join us

over here. 'It's sooo Aussie for the men and women to segregate at barbecues, but not here, hey Rose?' The women laughed, rearranging themselves at the table to make room for the men. Max was last there and sat at the end. Meggie pulled up a chair beside him. Angus looked at her, one eyebrow raised. He watched Meggie lift her chin slightly. 'I need to be close to the kitchen.' Then she turned to add a comment to the conversation Harriet and Debbie were having about tourism.

'Dad! We need a fieldsman, and more batters.' Billie was standing at the bottom of the steps, hands on hips. Tommy and Tiffany were at each end of the pitch, bats in hands. Drum threw up his hands, looking at the other adults. 'We've been called up to play.' He pushed his chair back and stood, calling to his daughter. 'Okay Billie, pick teams, we've still got a half hour before it's too dark to play.'

Billie and Tiffany were captains. Max was pleased to see Tommy was Billie's first pick. Drum, Harriet, Max and Meggie joined her team, while Tiffany had Ben, Angus, Jamie, Rose and Melanie. Debbie laughed, saying she'd feed Warwick and Charlie their dinner, 'it's a tough job but someone has to do it.' Rose skipped past her to the lawn, giggling over her shoulder, 'good luck with that Debbie, I'm here if you need backup.'

The game was hilarious, Max hadn't laughed so much in ages. Tommy and Billie bowled to Tiffany and Melanie, with Jamie catching Melanie out after only two runs. She excused herself to help Debbie with the little ones, so Ben stepped in, to bat. At one point Max was running backwards to catch a ball and almost landed on Rose. They high-fived, brushing themselves off, before re-joining the game. It was a short over, and their team went to bat. Tommy and Billie started, making more than a dozen runs before Angus caught Tommy out. They cheered from the sidelines and by the time it got so dark they were having trouble finding the ball Meggie hit out of bounds. They gave the game up then, all collapsing on the grass or the veranda steps, seeking cold drinks.

Melanie and Debbie returned, announcing the little ones were asleep, and it was time to light the barbecue. The game had broken the ice, if there had been any to begin with, and the conversation flowed. Max had expected the three children to eat first, or at least at their own table, but was delighted when he counted the chairs around the big table, realising they were not just included, but welcomed.

Meggie asked Tommy about his visit to see Rose's horses. He was wide-eyed and serious, explaining he had patted Cotton and Calico and even said hello to the old stallion, Topper.

Angus looked across at Max. 'You may have to consider investing in some horseflesh, Max, if you stay on here.' It was the first time he'd alluded to Max staying beyond the three month contract and his heart beat a little faster with the possibility.

Ben laughed. 'I'd like to see how you and Tommy manage in the flat behind the clinic with a horse as well.'

Meggie turned to him, an overly innocent expression on her face. 'Oh Max if you're going to get a horse you'll need a dog too.' Max suddenly saw the look on Tommy's face, excitement and awe, and thought he'd better temper the conversation before his son burst.

'They're teasing us a bit Tommy. But if we stay, then we'll look for a bigger place, with room for animals.' Tommy's excitement was obvious.

'Scuse me Angus.' Tommy was looking across the table, and suddenly all chatter stopped. Max wasn't sure what his boy was going to say, and he felt his heart begin to pound. 'My Dad is a really, really good Vet.' He nodded solemnly as he spoke. 'So you'll want him to stay. Us. You'll want us to stay. I'll help before and after school too, you'll see, you won't want us to leave.' Max closed his eyes for a moment, what should he say? He didn't want to upset Tommy and he didn't want to put Angus on the spot like that.

'Well Tommy,' Angus began. 'It's like this. I can already see that your dad is a really, really good Vet and I think we work well together. I wasn't one hundred percent sure, but since you've been helping with the patients in our animal hospital, I'm convinced that you both should join the practice permanently.' Tommy clapped his hands, then pushed his chair back, rushed around to Angus and threw his arms around him. Max was shocked and hadn't a clue what to do or say. He looked from Rose to Meggie, saw their happy smiles, and back to Angus. Over Tommy's head, Angus added, 'And we've already got a succession plan, Tommy here is going to be a Vet too.' He laughed loudly, giving Tommy a hug. 'We've no idea about Charlie's aspirations however.'

Suddenly everyone was laughing and talking at once, with Angus reaching across the table to shake Max's hand. More quietly he said, 'We'll talk Max, next week. But I mean it. I want you to stay.' Max could only mouth 'Yes and thank you.' Tommy returned to Max's side grinning broadly as everyone congratulated them and shook their hands. Max felt a lump of emotion in his throat and was relieved when Tommy asked to go to the bathroom. He took the opportunity to leave the room with him, needing to draw a breath and compose himself, but he risked a quick glance at Meggie as he went. Her look was almost pensive, but she had a small smile playing around her mouth, and she cocked a cheeky eyebrow at him. He hugged Tommy to his side as they walked down the hall. 'So we're staying mate. We'll work it all out next week, but we're definitely staying.'

'I knew he'd want us Dad. Tiffany already told Billie that her Mum said we'd stay.' Max glanced at his son. It was a good move for them. He sent Tommy back to the table while he took a moment to splash his face with cold water. He wasn't sure exactly what steps would be next. Sell the house in Newcastle, look for a place big enough to keep a couple of horses, but close enough to town for the clinic. And move on from the past. Put Liliana's death behind them, start living again. He was ready. They both were. They'd been in a state of limbo for almost a year, but he was determined to change that. He pulled his phone out of his pocket, looked at the last message he'd sent. Still no response. He sighed. There were things he needed to put right, and it was time he was more proactive about it.

Back at the table, the plates had been cleared and the children were playing a noisy game in the garden of 'chasey in the dark.' Rose and Meggie brought out plates of pavlova with lashings of cream, and they sat back, discussing everything from local Council, Drum was a Councillor, to small business and the property market. Ben Evans and his father were leading real estate agents in the area and Ben mentioned he had a couple of listings Max might like to consider, when he was ready. The girls seemed to be having a separate conversation, now grouped together at one end of the table, about the wedding. It was only three weeks away and he overheard Rose and Debbie oohing and aahing over the theme and planning, which Meggie was apparently in charge of. He wondered about Meggie for a moment. She must be around thirty, absolutely beautiful and if the conversation was anything to go by, professional and hard working. He wondered why she wasn't married or partnered. Perhaps she had someone back in the United States, although she had told him the evening before that she wasn't going back. Perhaps she was harbouring a broken heart? He should tread carefully, she was Angus's sister. He'd hate to mess up the opportunity by making a social faux pas.

The children finished their game, Tommy now perched beside him, his eyes drooping. Max looked at his watch, almost ten, they'd better take their leave. Tiffany was on Ben's lap, her head against his shoulder. Billie still seemed wide awake, but she sat beside Harriet, holding her hand.

Jamie collected Warwick from little Charlie's room and speaking quietly, they all made their way out to the cars, saying goodnight and thank you and see you on Monday. As the others drove out, Max put Tommy in the car, then turned to Angus and Rose, who stood side by side, Angus with his arm around his fiancée's shoulders.

'Thank you Rose, for the invitation, for including us today.' He tried to keep the emotion from his voice. 'I'm sure

Tommy will announce tomorrow that today was his Best. Day. Ever.' He tried to make light of it, but he was deeply touched by their faith in him, and their genuine welcome. Meggie had followed them out, now standing next to Rose. Max wasn't sure whether he should shake Rose's hand, but she stepped forward, drawing him into a tight embrace, saying simply, 'Welcome to Barrington Max. You and Tommy.' He hugged her quickly, then turned to Angus. He shook his hand, then found himself in a one-arm embrace. Angus released him. 'We'll nut out the details Max. I was planning to discuss this with you in the office next week, but I didn't want to wait when Tommy asked me the question. I hope you didn't mind.'

Max shook his head, 'I'd already decided I'd accept if you offered to make it permanent. We love it here. I'm glad you answered Tommy honestly. It really has been the best day, for both of us. Thank you.'

'Don't thank me mate, I'm grateful we found someone that's such a good fit for the practice, and for the area. Barrington suits you.' He took Rose's hand, glancing for a moment at his sister, still standing by Max's car. 'Goodnight, see you Monday.' They walked back to the house and Max turned to Meggie.

'It's been a lovely night Meggie, thank you.' He glanced into the car. Tommy was asleep in the front seat. He wondered if he should hug her, but she gave nothing away, so he looked at her for a moment. Long-limbed and beautiful, he wanted to kiss her.

'I have one complaint, though.' Her voice was low, a sultry tone he hadn't heard before.

'What's that Meggie?' He took half a step closer.

She leaned toward him, one hand touched his shoulder. He held her hand there with his, his heart pounding. She almost breathed the next words to him. 'I really wanted to spend all night talking to you. Just you.' She turned her face up and he leaned down, brushing her lips with his.

'There will be talking Meggie Hamilton. You heard your brother. We're staying. You're staying. There will definitely be,' he kissed her again, lingering this time, the slightest pressure of his mouth on hers, 'talking.' He walked to the car and looked back. She stood there, one hand raised in farewell, the other, fingertips on her mouth.

19

A ngus and Rose were washing up in the kitchen when Meggie returned to the house. She rushed out to the veranda, to collect any dishes or glasses still out there, and if she was honest, to feel the cool air on her face.

'Meggie. We've got it all. Come inside.' Rose stood at the door, looking at her fondly. She took Meggie's hand and led her back to the kitchen.

Angus had his back against the kitchen bench, his arms folded. 'You're a grown woman Megs and it's not for us to interfere. We can see there's a connection between you and Max, and we like him. And Tommy. I'm offering Max the opportunity to buy into the practice, so once he does, he'll be staying. But we all know he's been through something, he's got baggage. So, take it slowly, be friends first.'

While she knew he'd say something, she was still

annoyed. He had no idea what she'd dealt with by herself in the last couple of years, she didn't need his advice. Or approval. 'I've been making my own decisions for a long time Gus.' She raised her chin. 'Not all of them good ones, but that's life, isn't it? I'm aware of Max's position with your business and I promise I won't do anything to jeopardise that. And you're right, there is a spark between us. But we have to work out what that means for us. He's older than you Gus, so don't underestimate either of us.' Her chin was high, eyes flashing.

Angus looked at her for a moment, then opened his arms. 'Megs.' It was quietly said, and she found herself in his arms, sobbing. He was rubbing her back. After a few minutes, she stopped crying, drew back and reached for a tissue, blowing her nose loudly.

'Ha, my delicate sister!' Angus laughed. 'You always did blow your nose like a honking goose.' She laughed with him through her tears, playfully hitting him on the shoulder.

'But Megs, is there anything you want to share? Rose already said she thought you'd had some trauma in Napa. Do you want to tell us? But no pressure.' Angus glanced at Rose, who'd been hovering nearby. She hugged Meggie. 'We love you Megs. Both of us. We want you to be happy. But if there's something holding you back, we're here. No judgement, just love.'

Tears sprang to her eyes again. 'Yes. Yes I would like to tell you. I've been stupid, I've made mistakes. I've hurt others, and myself.' She looked at them both. 'More than you can imagine.'

They hugged her between them, and she let out a deep sigh. She looked at her watch. 'It's almost eleven, you must be exhausted. Yes, I will tell you what happened in Napa, but not tonight. I'll think about it over the next few days, and we'll talk.' She paused. 'Although this isn't something I want to share with Mum, and she'll be here tomorrow.' She kissed Angus on the cheek, hugged Rose again, and picked up her tote bag. 'But I feel better having said I'll share, I wasn't sure if I ever would. Thank you both.' Meggie walked to the door, looked back. 'I love you too. Both of you. And Charlie. So much.' Her voice broke as she spoke, and she ran to her car.

* * *

MEGGIE MADE SURE SHE WAS AT THE HOMESTEAD BEFORE HER Mum and step-father, Helen and Barry arrived for lunch, helping Rose with last minute details. She hadn't met Barry and liked him straight away. He had grown children and grandchildren of his own, and she was impressed with how easily he wrangled little Charlie. They made a good team and Meggie discovered she was genuinely happy for her Mum to have found someone at this stage in her life.

Meggie surprised her mum when she told them she wasn't returning to Napa and looked for a moment like she wanted to argue with her about it. But Barry put his hand gently over Helen's at the table and gave her a look. She said no more, and Meggie was grateful. Angus and Rose supported Meggie too, saying how lovely it was to have her so close after years on different continents. Meggie could read her Mum well, relieved to see she was appeased. Thankfully, the antics of Charlie distracted her.

Meggie stayed for dinner, Helen asked about the wedding arrangements. Rose and Meggie gave her an overview and she was delighted by the simple elegance. Towards the end of the meal Helen asked about the wedding dress.

'What style have you chosen Rose? You're tall and slim, I'm sure any style would suit you.' Helen took a sip of her wine.

Meggie jumped in. 'The bride never reveals her dress and certainly not with the groom present.' Rose looked relieved, Angus curious. 'So no hints about the dress at all, but we *can* tell you, in keeping with the simple elegance of the event, Angus will be in black tie.'

Helen accepted this, clapping her hands. 'Ohh, formal, Angus will look so handsome in a dinner suit.' She turned to Barry, patting his knee. 'And so will you Baz, I brought your dinner suit and your good grey suit, just in case. You'll look very distinguished too.' She leaned across to Rose. 'I've brought two outfits, to make sure I don't clash with your bridal party. You can tell me which one, later.'

'You'll look gorgeous too Helen. Mother of the groom. But yes, Meggie and I can choose the one that will work best in the photos.' Rose gazed around the table happily.

Stifling a yawn, Meggie excused herself. 'We had a barbecue here last night Mum, it got a bit late. I'm off, but I'll meet you for coffee in town tomorrow, just let me know when you're coming in.'

Meggie drove back to her apartment, tired certainly and a bit drained from her mother's questions, but she admitted it was lovely to be in the same room with her family for the first time in years.

Upstairs in her flat, she glanced across the street to the clinic. It was Sunday, and closed, but she thought she may have caught a glimpse of Max and Tommy.

20

Already hot at eight, Max looked at his son while they ate their breakfast cereal. 'Want to go down to the river today? We can swim, or even check out the kayak hire place, go for a paddle.'

'A paddle and a swim Dad. Tiffany said the river is running well and her dad, well, step-dad, took her and Billie down in a kayak last weekend.' He shovelled the last few mouthfuls of cereal in, rinsed his plate at the sink then announced he had to brush his teeth and he'd be ready to go.

Max took his time, tidying the tiny kitchen, finding their board shorts and packed drinks, snacks and sunscreen into a backpack. 'Okay, let's go. There's a kayak and a river waiting for us.'

Later that afternoon, they returned home hot and happy. Max had been impressed with how quickly Tommy mastered the kayak, and they'd ended with a swim and a picnic down near Rocky Crossing, where Drum had told them the best swimming spot was. Tommy sat on the sofa, after his shower, to finish some homework before school the next day and Max went through to the clinic hospital to check on their only patient, a border collie with a large litter of pups.

While he worked Max thought about the last few weeks. Moving to Barrington had propelled him into a forward motion, after treading water for so long. Tommy was happy at school and Max knew the Vet practice would be a good long-term investment for him, and if Tommy fulfilled his current dream to become a Vet, for his son too.

They'd go back to Newcastle next weekend, speak to the real estate agent about listing the house. He'd originally thought he'd hang on to it, he'd definitely get a capital gain in the city, and rent in Barrington. But in his heart Max knew he was committed to stay, so he'd ask Ben Evans for a list of prospective properties and once the house sold, he'd be ready to buy. There was something else he needed to do when they went back, and he'd been putting it off for too long. Max sighed. That part of the trip might be hard. It would certainly raise some difficult memories and emotions.

Later that evening, he relaxed on the sofa. Tommy was already asleep, and Max flexed his shoulders, thinking he'd be a bit sore tomorrow from today's exercise. His mind turned to Meggie. Stunning woman, smart and independent too. She'd travelled, worked all over, but still had a bit of Aussie country girl about her. It was her attitude really. He saw it in Harriet and Debbie too, and Melanie to a lesser extent. His logical mind told him that Meggie may have romantic baggage, and he wondered what her story entailed. The connection between them, the attraction, was obvious, but was she looking for more than that? Was he even ready for that himself? He had some loose ends to fix, to feel whole again. And he should be careful, Angus is her brother and he'd hate to jeopardise the budding friendship and business relationship with a romantic mis-step. But her eyes, when he kissed her, as fleeting as it was, hinted at a deeper passion. If he was honest with himself, her untapped depth fascinated and terrified him, and he couldn't wait to kiss her again.

He took his empty glass to the kitchenette and looked around ruefully. How was he going to explore a relationship, living in a one room flat? He chuckled quietly. He had time. They had time. little steps Max, little steps.

THE WEEK FLEW BY, THE CLINIC WAS BUSY WITH ANGUS MAINLY handling the large animal work, although Max joined him some afternoons, taking Tommy with him after school. They'd had a business meeting on Tuesday afternoon, Melanie had taken Tommy and Tiffany to get an ice-cream after closing the clinic for the day.

The offer from Angus was better than Max had expected. Full partnership in the whole practice, with Max running the clinic full time. The price was little more than he had received for his quarter share in the city business.

'It's up to you Max, you can open the clinic longer hours if you think the work is there, although Melanie still wants to work school hours. But it's important you do some of the farm visits with me, and for me when I'm away, just as I need to keep my hand in with the clinic to an extent. We need to be able to take a break from the business.' Angus handed a bound document to Max.

'I've written a business plan, with Rose's help I might add.' Angus looked sheepish. 'If you look at the projections, next year I'd planned to have a part-time trainee Vet. There's a local, Freddie, who's studying in Newcastle at the moment, keen to do all the prac work here.'

Max studied the projections, looking back at the earnings for the last two years. 'It's do-able. When will he be in town next? Maybe we can invite him in for a chat?'

Angus laughed. 'Freddie's a girl! Frederica Campbell. She's worked here in the school holidays for a couple of years, but now she's in second year at Uni, she'll be even more useful. She's filled in out the front for Melanie too, when she's on leave.'

Laughing with him, Max looked again at the projections. 'There's a couple of new pieces of equipment we could use in the hospital.' He pointed to a column of figures. 'Even after we pay ourselves we'll have profit this financial year, with a contract signed between us within the next couple of weeks. What do you say to some capital expense before the end of the financial year? We'd get instant tax write offs, which would help offset the injection of my capital.'

'You're right Max. Let's get some reps out here to quote.' Angus frowned for a moment. 'When I first bought the practice the area was in drought, the whole town was struggling, but especially the farmers, and profits were low. In fact, a lot of clients paid me in-kind. It's how I started my beef herd. I'd like to quarantine some of your capital into an interest-bearing account, to call on if we run into hard times again.'

'Okay. Agreed. That's sensible.' Max looked at Angus. 'But mate, you need to pull some of my investment back into your personal account, you've put in the hard yards, running this by yourself with barely a break for the last few years.'

'Oh, I will. Honeymoon money.' Angus chortled. 'We're going to Scotland.'

Melanie returned with Tommy, congratulating Max on the partnership. She gave him a shy hug and he was warmed by her pleasure at him joining the firm. Tommy ran through to the hospital to check the pups, they were going home tomorrow. If Max had space, he would have offered to buy one from the owner for Tommy. There'd be time and other pups.

'HOW ABOUT A PUB MEAL TONIGHT TOMMY? WE CAN CELEBRATE. Barrington Veterinary will have a new partner, officially, in about two weeks. But we agreed on everything today.' Max knew he was grinning madly, by the excited response from his son.

'Sure Dad. Tiff and I did our maths homework at the café already. I want a schnitty.' Tommy charged off to have a shower and change. Max picked up his phone, sending a text before he had time to consider if it was a good idea.

Barrington Vet and son request your company at pub for dinner.

A minute later his phoned beeped.

Barrington Weddings and Events accept. See you at 6.

New business name?

Yup. Registered today. Double celebration.

'Come on Tommy, don't use all the water, your old man needs a shower too!' Max's step was light as he walked to the bathroom door.

21

His face lit up when she walked in, there was a bottle of champagne in an ice bucket on their table. Sliding into the seat opposite the Masters men, she winked at Tommy.

'There are three champagne glasses. Are you joining the celebration? Why wasn't I invited to your eighteenth birthday?' She laughed as Tommy giggled.

'I'm not eighteen, you're silly Meggie. I've got lemonade in mine.'

'Of course, I am silly.' She looked up, meeting Max's eyes. Her stomach fluttered at the hungry look he gave her. He was one hot Dad. Hot Vet. Hot Max.

Max handed her a glass, raising his, she saw his smile reached his eyes, making them crinkle at the corners. 'Here's to Barrington Veterinary and Barrington Weddings etc.'

'Barrington. Place of new beginnings.' She responded. Her eyes focused on his as they took their first sip. A shiver of excitement ran down her back. She saw him sip, swallow, then swallow again. Good. He felt it too.

Tommy had taken a gulp of his lemonade, but was studying the menu, completely unaware of the frisson of tension between the adults.

'I'll order if you know what you want.' Max pushed the menu toward Meggie.

'What are you having Tommy?'

'I'm having the schnitty. It's got pineapple topping today.' His enthusiasm was infectious.

'I wouldn't normally, but I am celebrating and, well, you know. Pineapple.' She winked at Max. 'I'll have what he's having.' Max grinned, and she lowered her eyes while she took another sip of champagne. Just as well Tommy was here. They had to speak in code and *keep themselves nice*, as her Mum often said.

The conversation flowed, though. Max asked her about her business start-up, and she asked him about plans for the practice. They included Tommy in the conversation, and he graphically re-told their kayaking story from the day before. Her heart melted when he said earnestly at the end of the telling, 'you need to come with us next time Meggie. They have kayaks for three and four people. You can sit at my end, I'll help you.'

Unexpected tears came to her eyes and Meggie hid behind her glass. 'I'd like that Tommy.' Was all she could manage.

At seven-thirty they strolled back to her place, Tommy walking a few steps ahead. Max brushed her hand with his and she caught his fingertips with her own, for a moment, then his enormous hand folded hers inside it and a small charge ran up her arm and lodged in her chest.

Tommy looked over his shoulder, his face a grimace. 'C'mon Dad, I need to go to the toilet.' He didn't notice their hands were clasped.

Max dug in his pocket, pulling out a set of keys. 'Here you go mate. Run ahead and open up, I'll just see Meggie safely inside.'

'Okay. Night Meggie!' They watched as Tommy crossed the road, looking both ways first, although there was no traffic at all.

Max guided her to the door of her building, leaning down, his mouth close to her ear, his breath hot. 'Open the door Megs, we've got about five minutes.'

The door opened inwards, they stepped in, and he closed it with his foot because his hands were already on each side of her face, his mouth on hers as he backed her against the wall of the entry. She opened her mouth, emitting a small moan, which only served to deepen his kiss. He had one long denim clad leg between hers and she involuntarily pushed her body against it. Her hands were around his neck, holding his mouth to hers as they kissed, hot and hard. He drew his head back for a moment, growled her name, then lowered it, kissing her again before nibbling her earlobe. She involuntarily thrust her hips towards his, moaning softly.

He let her go and stepped back, so suddenly she almost slid down the wall. 'Meggie. We need to go slow.' He looked at the back of the door. Opening his arms, he drew her to him again, hugging her gently. That was even sexier. 'There's Tommy. And we need to talk. There are things that should be said. Before. Before we do more of this.' He was breathing hard, she could see him struggling to keep himself in check.

She had trouble forming words. 'Talk. Yes. We should talk. I have stuff. We should definitely talk.' Taking a deep breath, she stepped back. 'Goodnight Max Masters. Thank you. For dinner.'

He opened the front door and stepped out, his eyes meeting hers as he closed it. She wanted to kick it open, drag him back in, but she gave him the look instead. The look that told him she wants him. He acknowledged it with a look of his own, and after he closed the door she sat on the bottom step for a moment, to gather herself. Her legs were like jelly and her heart was racing. She was warm in places she'd forgotten she had.

MEGGIE SPENT THE MORNING WITH HER MUM, WHO DECLARED she loved the apartment, and took her across to Evans Real Estate to meet Harriet and show her the office she'd set up in the rear of their business.

The three of them walked down to the coffee shop for an early lunch. Meggie knew her independent attitude irritated her mum sometimes, but the morning was fun, and she thought maybe she was maturing, and her mum was relaxing. That made her chuckle. And having Harriet with them broke the ice.

Debbie, at the café, gave them special attention and Meggie could see her mum was impressed by the friendliness of those she met. Meggie felt validated, she'd made the right choice not to go back to Napa.

Walking back, they popped into the clinic. Melanie looked flustered, there were several people with their animals in the waiting room, and at that moment Angus stepped out of the surgery.

'Hi Mum, Megs. Harriet.' He looked harried. 'Max had to dash to Newcastle right after he opened this morning. A family thing, he said so I was a bit late starting.' He indicated the busy waiting room. 'No time to chat, sorry.'

'No problem son.' Meggie saw her mum frown as she spoke.

They turned back to the door, then Meggie strode up to the counter. Angus was already in the surgery with a client. 'Melanie, what about Tommy? Did he go too?'

'No.' Melanie leaned forward, her concern obvious and Meggie could see the people sitting closest in the waiting room were straining to hear. 'He was upset. Got a call from someone, said he had to go. Right now. So I told him to leave Tommy, I'd take him home with me. He can pick him up later tonight, or whenever he gets back. He was so relieved, Meggie, I could see it on his face.'

'Okay, thanks Melanie. If he stays away more than tonight, I can take Tommy if you like.' Meggie patted her hand, then walked through the clinic to the street, catching up with Harriet and her mum.

'I hope this Max is going to be reliable. Angus can't have him dashing off at the drop of a hat when he's on his honeymoon.' Her mother's lips were pursed, her displeasure obvious.

'It's a family emergency, Melanie said. Family comes first mum, you taught us that.' Meggie knew her tone was a bit sharp, but she was worried for Max, and wondered who, or what, could make him rush off like that. He always seemed so solid, dependable.

Harriet offered to drive Helen back to Barrington Homestead, said she had some wedding stuff to discuss with Rose. Meggie was grateful, she needed time to think. She'd message Max as soon as she was alone.

By seven that night she hadn't heard from Max. He'd given a thumbs up to her *are you alright?* message, but no more.

Around nine, she decided she'd go to bed. Melanie was keeping Tommy with her overnight. She wandered to the window overlooking the street, wondering when Max might come home. She was about to draw the curtain when she saw a faint glow from the clinic, like an interior light had come on. Max must be home. He's checking the animals.

She grabbed her keys and ran lightly across the empty street, down the side lane to the door of the flat. She was about to knock but knew if he'd gone through to the clinic he wouldn't hear her. She tried the door, it was unlocked. She stepped through the flat to the door to the practice. She did it quietly, cautiously, as it occurred to her that maybe someone else was inside. Angus most likely, looking in on the patients.

The light was coming from the hospital section, through a glass panel in the swing door. She stepped up to the door, looking through the window, then drew back in shock. A young girl was sitting on the floor, her face buried in the fur of a puppy. Meggie didn't recognise her at all.

She pushed the door open, and the girl looked up. Her face was tear-stained, she blinked once or twice.

Meggie stepped into the room. 'Hello. I'm Meggie. Who are you?' Her tone was soothing, yet wary. While the girl only looked about fifteen, she could be a thief, looking for drugs and side tracked by the puppies.

The girl raised her chin. 'I'm Indiana. My dad works here. I'm allowed to be here.' Her voice shook and she started to get up. Thoughts raced through Meggie's brain. Her dad? Is she Angus's daughter, someone she's never heard of, or Max's?

'Hi Indiana. That's okay. Who is your dad? My brother Angus owns the clinic here.' Meggie tried to keep her voice calm. The girl still looked frightened.

'Max Masters. He's my dad.' She buried her face in the puppy's fur again, before opening the enclosure and returning it to its mother and siblings. 'I can't find him. He should be here. My brother Tommy too.' She started to cry. 'I need to speak to him, I need to tell him the truth.'

Meggie was surprised more than shocked, but the girl was distressed so she stepped forward, holding her gently while she cried.

'Max went to Newcastle this morning and Tommy is staying with a friend. Family thing he said.' She grabbed some paper towel from a cupboard, handing it to Indiana. 'I expect that might be about you.' She raised an eyebrow.

Indiana nodded. 'I ran away. Last night. I was coming here. To tell him.' She sniffed loudly.

'Does he know that? That you're here? Have you messaged him?'

Indiana shook her head. 'My phone went flat. I forgot to bring my charger.' She looked up. 'Do you have one? A charger?'

Meggie placed an arm around Indiana's shoulders. 'Let's go to my place. It's across the road. We can charge your phone, and I have your dad's number, we can let him know you're here and you're safe.' She walked her from the clinic, turning out the light, then through the flat to the street. 'How did you get in? I'm curious.'

Indiana wiped her tears, her mouth curving upwards for the first time. She was pretty, fine bones, looked a bit like Tommy. Meggie couldn't see her father in her features at all. 'He always forgets to lock the door, I tried it, in case, and it opened.'

Across the street, Meggie took Indiana through to the kitchen. 'You must be hungry. Vegemite toast? Scrambled eggs? I can make a hot chocolate.'

'Can you call him? Tell him I'm here. Please?' Indiana handed her phone to Meggie, who put it on the charger.

Getting her own phone out, she found Max's number. 'Do you want to speak to him yourself?'

Indiana shook her head, her face anguished. 'I have to tell him in person. Can you ask him to come here? Please.'

'Okay. Why don't you go and find the bathroom, wash your face. I'll call him now.' She watched Indiana leave the room.

Max picked up after two rings. 'Meggie, I want to talk to you, but I can't right now.' He sounded distant, breathless.

'Don't go Max. Is it about Indiana? Your daughter? She's here. She's with me.'

There was silence for a moment, then Max's voice, sounding muffled. 'She's there? With you? She's safe?' He sounded close to tears.

'She's safe. I found her at the clinic, looking for you.' Meggie spoke quickly, hoping to ease his mind.

'Can I talk to her?' His voice broke as he spoke. He was struggling.

'I'm sorry. She wants to talk to you, but not on the phone. Says she has something to tell you, but it has to be in person. Can you come home?'

'I'll come now. I can be there before midnight.' He was silent, she wondered if he was still there. 'Meggie. Thank you. Keep her safe. Tell her I love her. Please don't let her leave.'

22

Max stopped at the service station at Raymond Terrace, getting fuel and a black coffee. He'd made another call before he left, then concentrated on driving. He thought a lot about what he needed to say to Indiana. And Meggie. She needed to know the full story too, if they had any chance of a future together.

He knocked on the door downstairs shortly after twelve. She must have seen him walk across the road because she opened it straight away. He wasn't sure what to expect from Meggie. Would she accuse him of lying about having a daughter? Would she be angry?

If she was angry, she didn't show it. She looked tired. 'Max. Come upstairs.' He followed her up, stepping into the living area.

'Indiana's asleep in the second bedroom. She was exhausted. But I told her I'd wake her when you arrived. She's really distraught.' Meggie led him to the couch, drawing him down beside her. 'I don't know what's happened between you Max, but it needs to be fixed.' She glanced away for a moment. 'I'll put the kettle on, make a pot of tea. Maybe you should gather your thoughts before you speak to her. Or we can wait until she wakes in the morning?'

Max leaned back, closed his eyes for a moment, then looked sadly at Meggie. 'I can't thank you enough Meggie. For finding her, keeping her safe.' He took her hand. 'I planned to tell you the full story, wanted to start, with you, with no secrets.' She squeezed his hand in acknowledgement.

'Yes, tea would be nice, thank you. Maybe we should let her sleep.' He watched as Meggie walked to the kitchen, heard the sounds of water running, then the kettle boiling. He may have drifted off for a few minutes, then she was beside him again, the tea things on a coffee table in front of them. He took the cup she offered, took a hesitant sip. Black and sweet. He glanced at her, 'how did you know I take it black?'

'You have your coffee black. I assumed. And you need the sugar, so I made it sweet.' She sipped her own as she spoke. She was calm, but he sensed underlying tension in her body.

He drank half the tea, then set the cup down. He took one of her hands and was relieved she didn't tug it from his grasp. 'Indiana is my step-daughter, she was six when I met Liliana. I've always considered her my daughter as much as Tommy is my son. I love her. Aways have.' He drew a breath. 'She spent time with Matthew, her biological dad, over the years, but she lived with us. Then, when Liliana died it all changed. I expected to keep her, keep the arrangement with Matthew for visits.' He leaned forward, his head in his hands.

He was struggling to keep his composure. He sat back,

looking at Meggie, his eyes burned with tiredness and unshed tears. 'But she hates me now. Blames me for her mother's death. For the car accident. Indiana was in the car with her, she saw her mother take her last breath. I can never make that right.' He sobbed, he couldn't help himself, and Meggie's arms were around him, rocking him.

He felt moisture on his cheeks. 'I'd found out she was having an affair. Liliana. With one of my partners. We argued. We'd been arguing a lot and I confess, I'd thought about ending the marriage too, before the affair. We weren't happy. But that day, she was taking Indiana to netball. I thought Indi was in the car, waiting, and I told Liliana it was over, I was leaving her. She walked out the door, slamming it. I looked up and Indiana was standing in the hall, crying, her water bottle in her hand. She'd come back in. She heard everything.'

He drew a breath. 'She never spoke to me again. Not at the hospital, not at the funeral. She went to Matthew and his wife. They arranged counselling. Nothing helped. She wouldn't speak to me or to Tommy. He hasn't seen his sister for a year. In the beginning he asked after her every day, but now he just looks sad sometimes and I know he's thinking about her, and his mum.'

He sat back, then saw Meggie turn her head toward the door to the bedrooms. Indiana was standing there, wearing a tee shirt he knew was Meggie's. Body aching, Max pushed himself off the couch, not caring that he was crying. He opened his arms as he walked toward her. 'Indiana. I love you.' He didn't know what else to say. 'I'm so sorry.'

Indiana threw herself into his arms and they collapsed on the sofa together, sobbing. Meggie started walking from the room. Indiana spoke, surprising him. 'Stay Meggie. I need you to stay.'

Indiana made room for her then looked at the ceiling for a moment. She turned to him. 'I don't hate you Dad. I don't blame you for the accident.' She started to sob, and Meggie rubbed her back gently, looking at him over his daughter's head, her face anguished, probably mirroring his own.

Indiana cried harder. 'The reason I don't blame you. Is. Because.' She hiccupped between words. 'Is because I killed her! I killed Mum! I took her away from all of us! From Tommy. He was only seven and I took her away from him!' She was almost screaming the words and Max and Meggie held her between them, rocking her.

He repeated, 'I love you Indi.' Over and over, until her sobs subsided. They were all crying. Finally, Indiana sat up and looked at him. 'Let me tell you dad. Let me tell you the truth. You may never speak to me again, but I have to say it.' He nodded. Meggie had her hand on Indiana's back. 'I heard what you said to Mum that day. About leaving her, about the affair. But dad, I knew already. I heard her talking to him days before, on the phone.' She straightened. 'She begged me not to tell you. Then, in the car that day, I yelled at her. I called her names, I told her I hated her. She was crying, telling me she loved me, that it wasn't about me. And she was driving fast. I didn't stop. I screamed at her over and over.' Indiana took a deep breath. 'She didn't see the lights change. She was looking at *me*. She drove straight through. I don't remember everything, someone pulled me out of the car. And I knew she was dead. I killed her dad.' He held her tightly, rubbing her back, murmuring to her.

Meggie left the room. After a while she came back, knelt in front of Indiana, a cup of hot chocolate in her hands. She spoke quietly. 'I've heard your stories, both of you. But I don't think anyone is to blame. Liliana was already upset when she got in the car that day Indi, and not necessarily because of the argument with you Max. Guilt is a powerful emotion. I expect Liliana was feeling plenty of that, just like you both feel guilty for her death. But she's gone, and you're still family.' He held her hand as she sat back on her heels. 'And think of Tommy, he needs you both. All I've really taken from tonight,' she waved her arm around them both, 'is that you love each other. As you should. Don't waste any more time on guilt. Guilt totally sucks.'

Indiana sniffed, then smiled tremulously at him. 'Guilt sucks Dad.'

'Oh Indiana. How I've missed you. Yes, guilt definitely sucks.' He kissed her forehead gently and was relieved when she kissed his cheek in return. A heavy weight was lifted from his heart, there was a way forward. It might not be easy, and he'd look into counselling, maybe together, but he had his girl back. He looked at Meggie. He saw how she handled them, how gentle and wise she was. She had a story to tell too, he was positive, and he would hear it, with the same openness she'd given him.

Looking at his watch, he said, 'it's almost two. We all need some sleep.' He looked at Meggie, but she spoke before he could ask her.

'Indiana will stay here. In the guest bed.' She nudged his daughter. 'We've got a girl thing going on here.' He heard Indiana giggle, she was looking at Meggie with open admiration. Meggie turned to him. 'You, Max Masters, can return to your man-cave and we will regroup in the morning. You need to pick Tommy up, he'll want to see his sister.'

'Yes please Dad. I saw your flat. It's tiny.' He laughed when she wrinkled her nose. 'Can I stay here for a couple of days? See Tommy. Look around a bit?' She hesitated. 'You've told Matt you found me?'

'Matt? You don't call him Dad now?' Was all he could think to say. She shook her head. 'You've been Dad as long as I can remember.'

He stood, said goodnight to Indiana. She went straight back to bed. He looked at Meggie. She jerked her head toward the door. He followed her downstairs to the entrance. There was so much he wanted to say to her, but he was exhausted, physically and emotionally.

'It's alright Max. Go home, get some sleep. Do you want to come here for breakfast, with Tommy, or meet at the café?'

'The café. Seven? I'll call Angus first thing, explain. I'll let Tommy have a couple of days off school.' Meggie nodded as he spoke.

'See you tomorrow Max.' She stood on tiptoe and kissed him softly on the lips. He let his eyes speak for him, then opened the door, stepping out into the fresh air.

23

Meggie was surprised when Indiana knocked on her bedroom door around six-thirty. They chatted a bit and Meggie made some green tea for them, before giving leggings and a San Francisco tee to Indiana to wear to breakfast. The tee was a bit big, but she loved it.

Indiana talked about her school, how she only had this year and next to go. She was interested in teaching but wanted to travel too. She asked Meggie about her career, where she had travelled. She talked about moving back in with Max and Tommy when they finished their three months in Barrington. Meggie wondered if Max would return to the city, change his mind about staying, if it meant Indiana would come home.

They walked down to the café together, Indiana peeking in shop windows and exclaiming over a display in a menswear store, about how old fashioned, but quaint, it was.

Meggie liked her, could see she'd need some guidance to overcome her feelings about her mother's death, one honest talk in the middle of the night wasn't a magic wand. But it was a good start.

They neared the café and Tommy burst from inside, his legs moving so quickly he was a blur. He threw himself at his sister. She leaned down, wrapping him in her arms. She was petite and he was tall, he was going to be a man-giant like his father, Meggie observed. They hugged, laughed and hugged again. He tugged Indiana to the counter, introducing her to Debbie, ordering his favourite milkshake for them both.

Max and Meggie sat together, watching. Max looked tired, but happy, he was grinning at everyone. 'I called Angus at six, gave him the abridged version. Melanie too when I picked Tommy up. Angus said to take as long as I need.' Max shook his head. 'He's a good man, your brother.'

'The best.' Meggie pushed her chair back, standing. 'Breakfast is on me today. I'll be back in a minute.' She walked to the counter. 'Two scrambled eggs with avocado on toast please Deb. And our usual coffees. Did the kids order theirs?'

'Tommy did. Pancakes for them both.' Debbie looked at her curiously. 'I take it Indiana is a bit of a surprise?'

'There's a story Deb. But it's going to be okay.' Meggie knew Debbie wouldn't ask anything further, but she also knew that she'd share some of the story with her, and Rose, Harriet and Mel, when they had some privacy.

Back at the table, Max was telling Indiana he was buying into the practice, staying in Barrington. Her face fell, for a moment. 'You can live here too if you'd like to Indi.'

'Your place is so small.' She appeared on the verge of tears. 'But I need to finish this year and next at my school. I'm doing really well Dad.' She looked at Meggie, then to Max. 'I thought you might come back.'

Max shook his head. 'I'm going to sell the house, buy a place here. With a paddock for horses.' Indiana seemed to perk up. 'Can I have a horse? I'll come on weekends when I can and in school holidays.'

'Of course. It'll be your home whenever you want to be here.'

Tommy interrupted. 'We're going to get kayaks too, we went down the river the other day, and I'm signing up for football, and cricket next summer. You can come and watch me play Indi.' Meggie liked the way Indiana gave her little brother a playful nudge. There was no need for Tommy to know what they'd been through.

They ate their breakfast, letting Tommy lead the conversation. Indiana was quiet, but Meggie thought she was processing. And she'd be tired.

'Dad.' That was Indiana. 'I'll stay today and tomorrow, if that's okay, have a look around. But I need to be back at school on Thursday or I'll fall behind.'

'Okay Indi. I'll speak to Matt, we can drive you home tomorrow afternoon, or we can meet him in Raymond Terrace.'

Indiana turned to Meggie. 'Can I keep your things for now?' She touched the neck of the tee.

'Of course. Keep them, I have heaps. And I'll wash what you had on yesterday, so you'll have a change of clothes. You can borrow a bikini if they take you for a swim.' Meggie looked fondly at Indiana, on the verge of womanhood, yet her childhood had been stolen when her mother died.

* * *

MEGGIE WAS FINISHING DINNER AT THE HOMESTEAD WITH ANGUS and Rose when Max pulled in on Wednesday evening. He asked if Tommy could watch television in the other room and accepted a beer from Angus. Helen and Barry had driven into the pub for dinner and Charlie was already asleep.

'Thank you. Angus, Meggie. Thank you for these last couple of days. I apologise for not telling you the full story. Telling you about Indiana. I honestly didn't know if she was ever going to speak to me again. And it was hard, thinking about that.' Max spoke quietly.

'It's all good Max. But I hope you haven't driven out here to tell me you've changed your mind about buying in?' Angus looked unsure as he asked.

'No. Not at all. If you'll still have me, I'm one hundred percent committed. Barrington is the right fit for us. Indiana is welcome to stay with Matt, but she knows she can come here for school if she prefers. We both love her, we've talked it over and we're happy for Indi to spend time with both of us. I don't expect her to make a decision like that in two days. And we'll be doing some more counselling.' He said this firmly.

'Whatever you need Max. If you need a day a week in the city, we'll work it out.'

Max continued. 'I'll be looking for a place of our own soon

enough. The agent says the current tenants want to make an offer on our old place.'

'Good. Speak to Ben. He'll have a few listings that may suit.'

'But don't worry about the animal hospital. Tommy and I can stay there when we have patients. Have a pub dinner.' Max gave a lop-sided smile as he turned down a second beer.

'We'll have Freddie here in the holidays, she might want to move into the flat.' Angus seemed more relaxed. 'There are always options, Max.'

Max seemed relieved. The look he gave Meggie across the table was questioning. They had a connection, but she really had to tell him her own story. It might be a deal-breaker and she'd rather know now.

Meggie spoke softly, and they all turned to her. 'There's something I've been wanting to tell you.' She glanced at Angus and Rose. 'And you too Max. You should know too.'

She was nervous, her hand shook as she picked up her wine glass, taking a sip. Rose said firmly, 'nothing you tell us will make any difference to us Megs. You know that.'

She spoke slowly, thinking about her words. 'I made some mistakes in Napa. Big mistakes, bad decisions. I fell in love with my boss about two years ago, we were away at a conference.' She inhaled deeply. 'He's married. We had an affair. More than an affair.' As she spoke, Max's face seemed to tighten. She pushed on. 'I knew it was wrong, but I thought.' She lifted her chin. 'I thought he loved me. Thought he would divorce her. He said he didn't love her anymore.' She wiped a tear from her cheek with the back of her hand. 'I fell pregnant. I was so happy, thought he'd divorce her for sure. We'd marry, have the baby.'

She looked at Max, his face had relaxed a bit, she wished she knew what he was thinking. Rose, beside her, was holding her hand. She was scared to look at Angus, afraid to see his disappointment. 'At the clinic, for the first ultrasound at twelve weeks, I saw his wife. She was pregnant too. About six months. She looked so happy.' She wiped another tear away. 'And that's when I knew. He'd played me. I was so stupid. He wasn't going to divorce her. Her father owned the vineyard. We'd even talked about starting our own one day, but maybe that was what *I* talked about, what *I* said.' She took the tissue Rose handed to her wordlessly. 'My work-mates had warned me in the beginning, tried to tell me what he was like. I didn't listen. I lost most of my friends over it. Because of my stubbornness. I resigned. Found another job.'

She looked at Angus, he was angry. God, she didn't want Angus to turn from her, but he needed to know. 'I thought about not having the baby. I was scared, alone. But I wanted her, I really wanted her. I was planning to call you, tell you I'd be home for the wedding, pregnant.' She shook her head, tears trickling down her face. 'I went into labour at five months. The baby, my daughter, only lived a few minutes.'

Angus stood, his face dark with anger. Meggie flinched as he stalked around the table to her. He pulled her out of her chair and enfolded her in his arms, his strength seeping into her. 'That bastard! I'd knock him out if he was standing here. That rotten bastard.' He held her while she sobbed. 'But Meggie, we would have welcomed you back, pregnant, with a baby, under any circumstances.'

'Really?' Relief began to wash over her. 'It was my own fault. My stupidity. I believed his lies, even though I was warned. I didn't listen.'

Angus growled. 'It takes two Megs. It always takes two. Don't be so hard on yourself.'

'I feel your pain Meggie.' Rose murmured. 'Losing your baby, your relationship, in another country, no family, feeling friendless. How hard this must have been.' Angus released Meggie. 'You could have told us Meggie. You could have come home straight away.'

Meggie blinked as more tears threatened to fall. 'I was being independent. I got myself into trouble, I was trying to work my way out of it. Coming home for the wedding was a lifeline, after losing her. I won't go back, I've travelled enough. I want to settle. Here. Close to my family.'

Max stood. 'You've been through a lot, Meggie, you're a strong woman. And I want to talk to you about this some more, but it's after eight and Tommy has fallen asleep on the couch, and I think your mum and Barry have pulled up outside.' Meggie felt relieved, that Max still wanted to talk. And even if her story cooled his ardour, maybe they could be friends.

The flurry of activity with Helen and Barry returning as Max carried Tommy, asleep, out to his car, allowed Meggie to hug Rose and Angus. 'Don't tell mum. I couldn't bear it if she knew.'

'You will tell her yourself one day Megs. When you're ready. Go home. Get some rest.' Angus kissed her forehead and walked her to the car.

24

Max tapped his hand on the wheel as he drove. Meggie's story had thrown him, momentarily. She's been through so much, discovered her partner was playing her, followed by the loss of her baby. Thinking about Meggie's kindness to Indiana, how good she is with Tommy, he was amazed at her strength and compassion. Yet logic told him he should slow down a bit, consolidate their friendship before embarking on a relationship. And he needs to be present for Indiana, and Tommy. They'd made a good start, finally he understood why Indi had cut them off, but the grief and guilt wouldn't instantly dissolve, and it will take time to help her through it. He had to put the kids first, as much as his body, and if he admitted it, his heart, finally free, yearned for Meggie.

So much to do, sell the house in the city, investigate properties locally. He sighed. Tommy woke as he pulled in behind the Clinic, and he walked him through to the flat, helping him undress and get straight into bed. He sat on the sofa for ages, thinking about the last few days.

* * *

WITH THE WEDDING LOOMING, HE WAS BUSIER THAN EVER. Angus was spending very little time at the Clinic and Max often returned to work after Tommy was asleep to research the new equipment they needed and check on their sleepover patients. On top of that Tommy had joined the netball comp with Billie and Tiffany and they trained two afternoons a week and had a game on Saturdays. Max was surprised, and pleased, that Tommy wasn't the only boy playing netball, it was a mixed competition, and he'd made friends with a couple of the boys from school now in the same team.

They'd had a weekend in Newcastle to see Indiana and sign the contract for the sale of the house. Indi had wanted to see Meggie, but she'd been in Sydney with Debbie and Rose, something about shoes and the bridesmaid outfit. Max was pleased Indi had asked after Meggie, she'd wanted to thank her and return her clothes, and he was even happier that Meggie had seemed disappointed it hadn't worked out to catch up.

Max had been surprised, and touched, when an invitation to the wedding was handed to him by Angus days after Indiana first appeared. It was for Max, Tommy and Indiana and he accepted with pleasure. He already felt an attachment to Angus, as a friend and business partner. He hired a dinner suit for Tommy, there was no point buying one, he would grow out of it in months. Indiana was a different story, she was petite and fair, and he wanted her to have something she would love wearing. In the end they chose a sky blue floor length gown, with shoe-string straps, fitted to below the bust, then fell softly to the floor. He thought they'd need to take it up, but she chose silver strappy heels and with the shoes on the length was perfect. He hoped she knew how to walk in them but chuckled when he remembered taking girls out when he was in his late teens. They all took their shoes off after a while anyway.

He wondered what Meggie would wear. She was tall, athletically built, she'd look stunning in any gown. He hoped he'd get a chance to dance with her. The thought of holding her in his arms, swaying to music, made his heart race.

He'd barely seen Meggie for more than a few minutes in weeks. Despite their minimal contact recently, he knew his feelings hadn't changed. If anything, they were stronger, now that he was finally beginning to sort through the aftermath of Liliana's death with his kids. He was impressed Meggie hadn't pushed for more contact, giving him space to spend time with Tommy and Indi when he wasn't working.

He knew she was hyper busy with last-minute wedding arrangements too and he wondered if she had chosen to remain friends, after processing all that came with him if a relationship started. His doubts niggled him at times. He was older than Meggie by six or seven years, and he had a family. After hearing her devastation at the loss of her baby, he was sure she'd want a child of her own at some stage. Could he offer that? He decided he'd leave the ball in her court. The thought had barely formed when she messaged him.

Any chance of a pub meal with the Masters men tonight?

Love to! See you at six. X

He tossed up whether to put the kiss on the end but pushed send before over-thinking it.

Tommy's hand waving caught his attention as she walked in. They were at their usual booth. Tommy slid over, making room for her beside him. Max leaned across and kissed her cheek before she sat down. He liked the way her neck turned pink when he did.

'What have you been up to Tommy Masters? I haven't seen you properly in weeks.' He watched her focus on his son, and sat back a bit, enjoying the conversation.

'I'm playing netball Meggie. With Billie and Tiff and the Bain twins. They're in my class at school.' Tommy was excited, he was loving her attention. But who wouldn't he thought.

'Have you played netball before Tommy?' Her interest seemed genuine, his heart sped up a bit. Beautiful, smart, compassionate. What's not to like? And sexy as hell, without even trying. He leaned forward a bit, to re-focus on the conversation. Tommy was speaking again.

'… not before I came here but I'm pretty good. We play at lunchtime. We beat the team from Stroud last week. I play centre 'cos I'm taller than the others. But Billie plays wing and she's super-fast and Tiffany is goalie. It's funny, she's usually really quiet but her Mum says she's a tiger on the court.' He giggled and Meggie laughed with him.

She nudged him. 'I bet you're all terrific. What's the best part for you?'

Tommy paused, his brow crinkled as he considered her question. She shot Max an amused look and he knew he was grinning back. Try as he might, he couldn't help it. 'Well, our netball team is sort of like …' he stopped and looked at Max, then turned back to Meggie. 'It's sort of like a family. I love winning and everything, but going to practice is really fun too, 'cos, you know…' he trailed off, looking uncomfortable.

Meggie leaned closer to him, but Max heard her clearly enough. 'Friends that are like family are the best Tommy. You know, it's quite likely you'll stay friends with these kids all your school years and even beyond.' She looked up, her eyes were glistening. Was she trying to tell him something? That she merely wanted friendship?

Changing the subject quickly, Tommy announced he was hungry. 'The duck spring rolls are on again tonight Meggie. Wanna share the entrée?'

'Duck spring rolls. Yes please!' she nudged him again, then glanced at Max. Then he saw it. Her expression was unguarded for a moment. Love. She loves Tommy. Meggie adores his son.

Emotion caught in his throat, so he cleared it before speaking. 'And for main course Meggie? And what about you Tommy?'

'Maybe a kids schnitty. But I always have that.' Tommy picked up the menu again, frowning.

'There's fish and chips on tonight. Whiting fillets. But the main course would be too big for me after sharing the spring rolls. How about we order the main and share that too? I'm sure they'll bring two plates if we ask.' Meggie was pointing to the specials board, and he laughed out loud when Tommy clapped his hands.

Max chuckled and as he got out of his seat. 'I'll order.

Wine for you Meggie?' She said, 'yes please' and he walked to the counter, ordered their meals and a steak for himself, then bought the drinks and returned. Tommy was talking about seeing Indi and having to wait around in *all* the dress shops while she picked a dress for the wedding.

'It's a girl thing mate, you'll get used to it when you're older.' Max raised his glass. 'To Angus and Rose.' He watched Meggie take a sip of her wine, a small smile playing around her mouth. Like she had a secret. He wondered what.

An hour later they walked Meggie back to her apartment, and despite offering the keys to Tommy to let himself into their flat, he announced he'd wait and walk home with his dad. If Meggie was disappointed, she didn't show it. She gave Max a cheeky look, like she knew he was keen for a few moments alone. So he said goodnight and kissed her cheek, then watched as she leaned down and hugged Tommy. He wondered if Tommy would pull away in embarrassment, but he threw his thin arms around her waist and hugged her tightly in return. It moved him beyond words, and as she straightened he placed his hand on Tommy's shoulder as the boy whispered, *'goodnight Meggie'* and they walked across the street. Max turned and looked back. She was standing there still, watching them. He raised his hand, and she raised hers in reply.

25

On the eve of the wedding Rose and Debbie slept over at Meggie's apartment. They shared a bottle of champagne and chatted until nearly midnight, when Debbie declared they all needed their beauty sleep. Meggie had been surprised, at first, that Rose and Debbie were happy to share the spare bedroom. Meggie had offered to sleep on the sofa. But as the night wore on, she got it. The women had been friends since school days and had shared a room many times, and she could see how their history and closeness, giggling like schoolgirls, made it more fun for them.

Meggie was first up, making healthy smoothies for breakfast, with a platter of fruit, nuts, cheese and dips to sustain them through the morning. The hairdresser and make-up artist were due at ten and the photographer at twelve. Rose and Debbie were being driven to Barrington Homestead at two in a nineteen-forty-seven white Daimler, in keeping with the theme. Meggie and the photographer would head to Barrington in her car, arriving ahead of the slow travelling vintage vehicle.

The morning was fun, and Meggie enjoyed watching the hairdresser turn Rose's thick auburn hair into an up-do. Rose didn't require heavy make-up, but they focussed on smoky eyes and bright red lips. Debbie's blonde hair was in a similar style and the navy-blue pinstripe dress fit her like a glove, the pencil skirt ending just above the ankles.

'You know I'll need help walking up the stairs at the homestead?' Debbie laughed, demonstrating how the narrow skirt made it hard to take more than a tiny step. Rose giggled, 'I'm sure Jamie can pick you up, if he needs to.'

Finally, they helped Rose into her gown. With her hair and make-up already done, she looked like a star from old Hollywood as she turned in a slow circle for the photographer. Meggie loved the way Rose grinned at Debbie, her eyes wide. 'Do you think Angus has any idea? About the style of the gown?'

'Not at all. He said something to Jamie the other night about you being a little conservative, and thought you'd have a full-length white gown, modern but modest.' They looked at each other and laughed.

'He's in for a surprise then!' Rose took Meggie's hand. 'Thank you, for organising this, I fell in love with the dress, but you've styled the whole day around it. Even the wedding car. Everyone will expect a white gown. I can't wait to see Angus' expression when he sees me.'

Meggie squeezed her hand back. 'He'll fall in love with you all over again Rose Gordon. And you know we're going to take some *first look* photos and video footage. He won't be allowed to look at you until you step fully out of the car, we'll have it arrive close to the outdoor chapel. When we give the signal, Jamie will tell him to turn around and we'll zoom in on his face. You know the rest, what you have to do.'

Meggie looked at her watch. 'You've got fifteen minutes before we leave. Sit for a moment while I quickly put my outfit on.' At Rose's insistence Meggie had her own hair in a similar style, and had help with her make-up, wearing a deep red lipstick. Secretly she thought it was a little bit Katherine Hepburn, and so was her outfit. She wasn't in the wedding party and had a lot of behind the scenes things to attend to. She hadn't shared it with Rose but hoped she'd like it.

Stepping back into the living area she cleared her throat. Rose, Debbie and the photographer turned as one. She watched Rose smile, look at Debbie, then laugh. 'You're perfect!' She turned to the photographer, 'a photo with my sister please.' Meggie's heart flipped over when Rose called her sister instead of sister-in-law. But she felt the same. Rose had become a sister to her too.

A couple of photos, then Debbie joined them. Meggie could see Rose bursting with happiness, but she didn't think it eclipsed her own. Standing there, with Rose and Debbie, laughing together, she realised she felt whole. And strong. She hadn't felt this way since before Napa. Actually, she didn't think she'd ever felt this good, ready to move on with her life. She wanted what Angus and Rose have. Is Max the one? Maybe. Tommy already filled her heart and she hoped she could build a relationship with Indi too, when they had more time together. She realised Max may not want to start another family, have a baby, he had a lot going on with his children already. Would it be deal-breaker for her? Maybe not. But if she didn't explore the possibilities with Max, she knew she'd be sorry. And she hoped they would have a friendship strong enough to withstand any outcome.

* * *

A ROSE-COVERED ARBOUR WAS SET UP IN THE GARDEN DIRECTLY in front of the grand old homestead that Rose's forebears had built. They had white folding chairs on either side of a red carpet aisle and Meggie had told the driver of the Daimler to take at least fifteen minutes to give her time to get the photographer in place for the *first look* video.

Harriet and Drum were acting as ushers, standing with the celebrant and Angus and Jamie in the arbour when Meggie arrived, parking her car to one side. As she helped the photographer with his gear, she heard Jamie say quite clearly, 'we'd like all of the guests to face us at the front after the car arrives before Rose gets out. No peeking, we want Angus to be the first to see the bride. So eyes front when we tell you, especially you Angus.'

Meggie stood to one side at the back, partially hidden by rose bushes. She could see Max on the groom's side, his back broad, with Indi and Tommy beside him. It looked like Tommy had a dinner suit too, so gorgeous. And Indi was in blue. Meggie saw her Mum in the front row, wearing deep green and gold. Little Charlie was squirming on her lap. She'd be dying to peek.

The Daimler pulled in and Jamie directed all eyes to the

front. Even Harriet turned around. Meggie watched as the driver opened the door for Rose. Jamie told Angus to turn around. She watched closely as her brother turned, then looked at Rose. She looked exquisite, almost regal. She carried herself with such grace. Meggie turned back to Angus, he staggered slightly, Jamie grabbed his arm. He was grinning, his face a picture of astonishment and adoration, then he wiped the back of his hand across his eyes. He mouthed 'I love you' to Rose.

Drum told the congregation they could turn. Rose walked slowly toward Angus, Debbie almost hidden behind her. Meggie heard the oohs and ahhs of the crowd, and murmurings and phones clicking. Halfway up the aisle Rose stopped, and turned in a slow circle, showing the almost backless design of the dress, held together by delicate rose gold chains. A few people clapped and someone let out a low wolf whistle. Rose kept her demeanour, taking the last few steps to Angus, placing her hands in his. The congregation turned then, to watch Debbie, a few steps behind Rose, her small steps, encumbered by the slim skirt, making her hips swing. Everyone clapped again and Jamie shook his finger at her. Meggie thought he mouthed, 'you're in so much trouble Debbie Tait.'

Debbie stood alongside Rose, and Drum and Harriet sat down on the bride's side, in the front row. The congregation were all focussed on the front and Meggie stepped forward, planning to slip into a spare seat a few rows behind Max. But he turned, saw her, and half stood up. He met her eyes. Something passed between them.

The celebrant began to speak.

26

Max had been searching for Meggie, she had to be there somewhere, stage directing the event from the side perhaps, so all attention would remain on Rose and Debbie. With everyone now looking at the wedding party, he sensed movement behind and turned his head.

He saw her. Meggie. Not wearing a gown at all. She had on navy pants, some sort of silky satin fabric, fitted snugly to her waist and hips but kind of loose legs. On top she had a white shirt, the same sort of fabric as the pants, but it was a man-style shirt, the collar up and sleeves rolled to the elbow, tucked into the pants showing off her small waist. The top buttons were undone, he could see her cleavage. She had her hair done in a similar style to the bride and dark red lips. He grinned, almost stood up. Classic. The look was perfect for Meggie. She had an hourglass figure, and the long pants made her look even taller.

He returned his gaze to the ceremony, then glanced about at the decorations. He hadn't been inside the marquee yet, but he was sure it was in keeping with the theme. Meggie had done a great job, she really has flair. Even the car looked the right vintage. He'd ask her later.

* * *

CANAPES HAD BEEN SERVED ON THE VERANDA WHILE THE BRIDAL party had their photos taken around the homestead. Tommy said they'd even gone down to the stables for a picture with the horses. Max had looked for Meggie then, but she had gone with the bridal party, probably directing the photographer.

Meggie joined them for the meal, they were on a table with Melanie, Ben, Harriet and Drum. It was the perfect table. Indi sat on the other side of Meggie, and they chatted a lot over the meal. Tommy, Billie and Tiffany had excused themselves after the main meal and were playing in the garden outside the marquee. They'd made him promise to call them in for dessert.

The official part was relatively short, although Jamie had them in stitches with his best man speech. His comments about the beauty of the bride and bridesmaid were heartfelt and Max had to cough to hide his emotion. He felt Meggie looking at him then. But kept his eyes to the front. One look, in that moment, would undo him.

Angus made a short speech, then held his hand for Rose to stand. She thanked everyone, but especially her sister Meggie, for putting the day together. He glanced at Meggie, a tear slid down her face. He took her slender hand in his and squeezed, then handed her his handkerchief.

The band struck up a waltz and Angus led Rose to the floor, dancing perfectly together, Rose elegant and sexy as she twirled with Angus. Debbie and Jamie joined them on the dance floor, Debbie having trouble with her skirt until Jamie picked her up in his arms, spun her around, then held her close, rocking slowly from side to side, making the watchers laugh. The waltz finished and the band changed to swing tunes, and within moments the dance floor was full. Meggie had left the table again, murmuring something about the cake, so Max asked Indi to dance with him.

He showed her how to do the jitterbug, and she giggled the whole time, flushed with happiness as he spun her around. Two songs later she said her feet hurt and he danced her back to the table, kissing the top of her head as she sat. He grinned when she pulled her shoes off, kicking them under the table.

Max was about to sit when Meggie reappeared. He took her hand wordlessly and led her to the dance floor, drawing her in, holding her firmly against him as he managed a foxtrot. He didn't want to let her go.

He murmured in her ear. 'You look stunning Meggie. Your outfit is perfect. It, um, shows off your ...' He paused.

She leaned back, laughing. 'My?'

'Assets. Your assets.'

'Really Max Masters? You've mentioned several times already, over dinner, how much you like my hair like this, and the outfit. I think you need some new material.' She laughed, then leaned in. 'You're devastatingly Clark-Gable-ish in the dinner suit by the way.'

He chuckled. He loved her humour, her playful side. They danced through another three songs, and he sang, slightly out of tune, in her ear. He knew all the old show tunes. He could feel the warmth of her body through the fabric of her outfit. If he wasn't in a public place, he'd explore a little more with his hands. As it was, he'd caught a glare from her mother Helen when one hand slipped below Meggie's waist, touching the top of her very shapely bum.

Tommy bounded onto the dance floor to tell them dessert had arrived, so they returned to the table. The younger kids ate theirs quickly then ran onto the dance floor, dodging in and out between dancing couples. Max looked over at Drum and Ben. 'Do we tell them to stop?'

Drum glanced at Billie, running back through the tent, Tommy and Tiffany behind her. 'No mate. They're fine. Let them have fun.' Max relaxed.

The others got up to dance and Indi went in search of the bathroom, and it was only Meggie and Max at the table. Their chairs were close, legs touching, as they spoke in each other's ears to be heard over the music. 'You've got great kids Max.'

'I know. I'm really lucky. So grateful to have Indi back, Tommy was missing her as much as his mum.'

Her head was almost on his shoulder. He kissed the top of her head, then leant down. 'But I don't think I'm finished.'

She looked at him, confused. 'Finished what? Dancing? My feet are sore.'

'Kids. I don't think I'm finished having kids.'

Now she looked at him, startled, but was prevented from

saying more as Jamie announced the bride and groom were leaving shortly. The guests stood in a large circle around the dance floor and Angus and Rose did a traditional country wedding goodbye, each working their way around the circle in opposite directions, thanking their family and friends for coming. The band played a soft waltz and guests chatted and laughed together.

Finally they were done, and Jamie jumped back on stage, saying into the microphone, 'the bride is going to throw the bouquet, ladies, get ready.' Max watched in amusement as the single women, and even the little girls stood together, shouting for Rose to throw them the bouquet. Meggie stood back from the group, Max a few steps behind her. Rose turned around and everyone counted down, then she tossed the bouquet over her head, high into the air.

It sailed over the heads of the noisy bunch of women and girls. Meggie reached up and almost touched a dangling ribbon as it flew by. Almost in slow motion it began its descent. Max took one step back and deftly caught it in his giant paw. The room fell silent. He looked at Meggie, his eyes drawing her to him. Almost in a daze, she stepped closer. He knelt on one knee, held the bouquet out to her. She took it, then threw herself into his arms and the room went wild, cheering and laughing.

She whispered to him. 'You said something about kids?' He kissed her for a full minute, ignoring the laughter and cheers around him. 'First things first, Meggie Hamilton. I'm coming home with you tonight. There are things to be said. And things to do.'

Rose and Angus were beside them, and he watched

Meggie fall into Rose's arms, hugging her tightly. Angus pumped his hand. 'Good work mate, good work.'

Rose and Angus stepped toward the waiting Daimler, taking them to Sydney for the night, then they were off to Scotland for three weeks. Rose whispered something to Meggie, then skipped back to Angus, sliding into the back seat before him.

'What did Rose say to you Meggie?' Max asked quietly.

'She wants hot news when she gets back. We've got three weeks.'

'Then we better start straight away.'

THE END

ACKNOWLEDGMENTS

A huge thank you to my writing friends, co-authors of the Love in a Sunburnt Land anthologies (Vol. 1 & 2) - Rhonda Forrest, Louise Forster, Leanne Lovegrove and Emma Powell. You're my Tribe, thank you.

Meggie & Max was written for Sunburnt Land Vol 2, and my fellow authors kindly allowed me some extra words. At 36,000 words, it's quite a bit longer than the 30,000 words we had agreed to. I just couldn't find it in my heart to edit anything out!

Thank you also to my daughters Jasmine and Emily for always being on Team Susan, giving me lots of marketing tips and suggestions for cover design.

Thank you also to Bloke, for believing in me without reservation! (Oh and shopping, cooking and being patient with all the time I spend in my writing room).

ABOUT THE AUTHOR

Susan Mackie is first and foremost a farmer's daughter. Her career as a journalist, small business owner, tourist resort developer, real estate agent and government employee created a wealth of experience from which to develop characters and storylines. Susan has two daughters and two grandchildren, and lives in a country town in southern Queensland with Bloke. Meggie & Max is the second novella in her Barrington series, which includes two full length novels. They can all be read as stand-alone's.

https://www.susanmackie.com/

ALSO BY SUSAN MACKIE

Charlie's Will

Barrington Series - Book One.

"A lovely rural drama with plenty of romance and steam..." Mandy White, Australia.

Rose Gordon knew the farm would be hers when her grandfather died.

Strong and sassy, Rose is the sole heir to five generations of cattle country and the magnificent Barrington Homestead.

But Charlie's will is not as she expects and the appearance of Angus Hamilton on the day of the funeral unsettles her. Handsome and single, she's attracted to him. But can she trust him?

The ongoing drought and discovering she has friends, if not family, in the small rural community complicate matters.

More sinister threats lurk in the shadows.

Will Rose give up city life to face the threats head on and fight for her inheritance?

A Place to Start Over

Barrington Series - Book Two

"Susan Mackie brings the town and its people alive ... the warmth of the characters flow from the pages like melted butter on toast." Mandie, Goodreads.

Can one bad decision change your life?

While recuperating from her biggest mistake, Harriet's had time to plan a fresh start, away from the city.

With a business plan on her laptop and determination in her heart, she leaves Sydney, heading north. It's a long drive and she's only just beginning to heal, so she's booked a stopover at Barrington Homestead on the way.

Harriet meets Drummond Murray on the road to Barrington. He's a cattle farmer and fifth generation local. Impeccable manners but not much warmth. She has no choice but to accept his assistance, but she's not keen to see him again.

In contrast, Ben Evans is a local stock and station agent, good humoured, warm and welcoming. Except Harriet isn't looking for romance and she's keen to continue her journey north. When circumstances conspire to keep her in Barrington after months of feeling helpless, feeling needed strikes a chord.

A cast of local characters and new friendships make her wonder if this might just be her place to start over.

Love in the Ragged Mountain Ranges

Barrington Series - Novella One

"Wow it was so so good. I highly recommend this book." Jane Giddings, Top 1000 Reviewer, Amazon

She swore she'd never trust again.

Buying the old courthouse near the Barrington Tops ragged mountain ranges was a fresh start for Nicole and daughter Lucy. Renovating the run-down building into a home and B & B accommodation would help them recover from the trauma they had endured. Nik promised Lucy it would be just the two of them. Always.

But the removal truck getting stuck in the driveway on the first day threw them into neighbour Robbie's path. He sorted the problem, then returned with son Harry to help them unload. Nik instinctively liked him, but she couldn't trust her instincts. And more importantly, she vowed to keep the promise she'd made to Lucy.